Drop Dead Gorgeous

Donald Churchwell

This book is a work of fiction. Names, character, places, and incidents are the products of the author's imagination or used fictitiously. Any resemblance to actual events, locals or persons, living or dead, is entirely coincidental.

Published by Donald Churchwell

DEDICATION

This book is dedicated to the men and women of the United States Military and our intelligence agencies. Many of these men and women leave their homes, families, and friends to travel to some God forsaken part of the world. They risk their physical and mental health, and their lives to stand between us and those who would do us harm.

Because of their sacrifices, we have the freedom to sit in our recliners and criticize them. Please join me in saying a prayer for them, and when you see a young man or woman in uniform, take the time to say "Thank You."

ACKNOWLEDGMENTS

I want to express my sincere thanks to the following people. All of you helped make this possible

Lora Mason. I couldn't have had a better cover model, just a fabulous job!

Alexis Renee De La Rosa. Thanks for a great graphics job on the cover

Devin for editing. Any mistakes are the author's!

HLH for reviewing the legal aspects in the hearing

Patrick for reviewing technical aspects of the military side

Bill at Jay's Gun Range. Thanks for the opportunity to shoot some of the off-the-wall weapons found in my books

Tomi, thank you!

Thanks to my wife, she indulges these books and the time I spend. She says the books are great; because I wrote them. What a fan!

Drop Dead Gorgeous

PROLOGUE

Fredericksburg, Virginia

November 1992

Alexandra Jane Moring put the finishing touches on dinner as she heard her mother, Samantha, pulling into the gravel drive to their home. Home was a hundred-and-fifty-year-old farmhouse in the country outside Fredericksburg. Alex's brother, T.D., would be out for the evening and so would her father. Tonight it would be just her and Samantha. An ideal scenario for a daughter-mother talk.

"Alexandra, whatever that is, it smells delicious!" Sam yelled from the foyer. Two or three days a week, Sam drove to D.C. to either spend time at her own office or go by her office at the *Washington Times*. "Your dad will be late tonight. They have some sort of minor crisis at the FBI Quantico office. He and Director Hendricks are meeting with some people from one of those other alphabet agencies. Where's your brother?"

She needed time to talk to Samantha one-on-one. "T.D. is at a friend's house, Mother. He'll be home later." A lot later.

"Thank you for making dinner, dear. Do I have time to change?"

"Certainly, Mother. Dinner will be on the table in about ten minutes."

Irritation crept into Sam's mind. Alexandra insisted on calling her "mother," yet she called her brother T.D. On the other hand, she did call Steve "father", so it wasn't just her. Sam kicked her heels off as she entered her bedroom, hers and Steve's bedroom. She loved their farmhouse. When the family had grown, they had made another addition. Since the farmhouse was so old, she'd wanted it to look properly done, so an architect had been hired, and a small army of contractors had worked for months. The result was a house totally unchanged from the front. The original foyer, sitting room, dining room, and Steve's office were identical to the original, other than modern wiring and discreet central air. The large, shaded front porch with the rocking chairs was untouched. Upstairs, however, was completely new. The finished product had resulted in a new bedroom for each child, a spare bedroom, and a new, large suite for her and Steve with a fabulous bath and even a small desk and office area for Sam. The downstairs had been popped out past the kitchen to include a screened porch and a mudroom. A pool and patio had been added outside for everyone to enjoy.

She quickly stripped off her suit and pulled on a pair of jeans and a Harvard sweatshirt. She headed downstairs to join her daughter for dinner.

She had been concerned about Alexandra almost from the beginning. Sam and Steve had even consulted with a leading child psychologist. Alexandra was almost certainly a genius. She had never caused a problem. Her physical characteristics were normal. She was tall at five foot seven, perfectly proportioned, and a born athlete. When it suited her, she could be stunningly beautiful. The problem was her emotions, or rather the lack of them. She hardly spoke, and when she did, she seemed cold, even distant somehow. Samantha didn't doubt that her daughter loved her family, especially her brother, but there was just an absence of the love one would expect a daughter to return.

"Would you like some wine, Mother?" Alexandra asked as she sat down. She had a bottle of wine and two glasses. "Do you think we could eat first, Mother, and then I was hoping we could talk?"

Samantha nodded; she bowed her head, praying silently that she would handle whatever was coming. Alexandra had made stew and rice with a salad. Sam was hungry, and the dinner was actually very good. "Alexandra, this is wonderful! Did you go to the store for the beef?"

"Actually, Mother, it isn't beef. This morning that meat was a nice doe I took with my bow at about forty yards. I dressed it and prepared it myself."

"Alexandra, I didn't realize you enjoyed hunting. Did Mr. Frank show you how?" Mister Frank, as they called him, was their farm manager. He was on the property most days; sometimes he and his wife stayed in the apartment in the barn.

"Partly. Father taught me the weapons. I can load, fire, and clean everything in his secret room. Mister Frank taught me…"

"Wait, secret room? Are you telling me you know about the room?"

"Of course, Mother. T.D. and I have known all about that stuff for years. That's what we need to discuss. We discovered the room, the other room behind the cabinet over there"—she nodded over her shoulder toward the old cabinet—"the surveillance equipment, everything. Don't worry. We didn't mess with the explosives or the hand grenades. We're bright, we're inquisitive. We've snooped and compared notes for years. We know most of what you and Father have been doing for years. Between Linda, Mr. Hendricks, and Chrissy, we've pieced together that our laid-back, mundane parents are anything but!"

"But, Alexandra, all your father and I wanted was for the two of you to have a normal childhood…"

"We knew that, Mother, and you have no idea the respect my brother and I have for how the two of you have struggled to do that. You have been in some of the highest offices and biggest conspiracies in the country for years. You've fought evil in your own way. What T.D. and I have decided is that both of you need to just sit back now. Enjoy each other, this farm, your jobs. That's what I wanted to discuss. I'm dropping out of Harvard. I intend to finish my degree at Vanderbilt because of their ROTC program, and then I'm joining the Marines."

"Oh dear God, Alexandra, your father will never allow it."

"Yes, he will. He was a Marine too. He wasn't happy about it when I told him, but he also realized, as of my next birthday, he can't stop me. He said he will give me his blessing, but only if I make it right with you."

"Oh, Alexandra, this is just so different from what we had imagined. You and T.D. are so brilliant I had just hoped you would graduate from Harvard, maybe law school. I wanted T.D. to go to M.I.T.; I even approached Stark Draper. He heads the computer sciences department. It's going to be the wave of the future."

"We realize that. T.D. is going to do just that. After the Marines for me, and T.D. learning everything there is to know about computers, the two of us will be ready. We're going to take the baton." Alexandra stood and walked to her mother. She urged her to stand and gripped her in a tight hug. “So, Mother, what’s it going to be? Are you on board? Will you and Dad let us take up the fight?”

“Dad? You just called your father dad. Why? Why am I mother?”

“He met my condition.”

“Which was?”

“Thomas David is T.D., always has been. I’m Alexandra. Always. I assume you’ve wanted to differentiate between the two of us. But T.D. calls me A.J. He couldn’t pronounce Alexandra. That’s the deal. Call me A.J. Alex would be okay sometimes.”

“That’s it?”

“Yep.”

“Okay. You have my blessing. You know what we’ve done, your father and I, has been dangerous. I’m going to be terrified.”

“We know…Mom…that’s the reason for the Marines. There are some skillsets that have to be learned by doing. But Dad says I have the basics, the instincts. He says those *can’t* be taught. We’ll make you very proud, Mom, you’ll see.”

“Alex, I love you. I love my family. I never had one, not really. But I know this; you and your brother are amazing. Your dad is too. I know you have issues with emotions, but for me, right now, please hug me again.”

“You got it, Mom!” They hugged in the kitchen for a long time. Alexandra poured the last of the wine into their glasses.

Samantha sat back down; something was bothering her. “Alex, I’m concerned. Now that I’ve thought about this, I can see you, you know…

“Killing someone, Mom?”

“Well, yes. But T.D.? I don’t see it.”

Alexandra downed the rest of her wine. "Don't worry. We've worked that out. I'm the doer; he's the thinker. He's the part of me that's missing. The conscience if you will. You have no idea how many times he's prevented me from beating the living shit out of someone that really needed it. I need him. At least until I find a T.D. of my own. 'Till then, we'll talk, often. Finish your wine; you look like you need it. This has all gone much better than I imagined. So you're in agreement with all this?"

"Really, no. Not totally, but I agree with your dad. It's going to happen, so we may as well deal with it. I am going to think about it, but we'll work it out. As a family, right, daughter?"

"Yes, Mother, as a family." Alexandra smiled.

CHAPTER 1

100 kilometers South of Cali, Colombia

"He's doing it again!"

"Chill out, LT, it'll be okay."

"It's fucking not okay, Vasquez. We've been out what, three times with Miller? He's got us lost all three times!"

Sergeant Vasquez looked at his immediate supervisor, First Lieutenant A.J. Moring; he tried to hide a smile. He'd been able to hear her teeth grinding when the Toyota Land Cruiser ahead of theirs took a right at a fork in the red clay road they had been bouncing down. At least he thought so.

The two-truck convoy had left their headquarters in Cali that morning. Lt. Moring and her unit were S-2, intelligence. They had been dispatched to a cocaine factory taken down by the Colombian Army with help from the DEA. Moring and Vasquez were in the front, and a corporal, "Dink" Moreno, and "Tom", a shady looking DEA agent were in the back. Their job was to collect any forensic evidence at the factory. That would include fingerprints, written or electronic data, and photographs of the deceased. The Colombian army had a security detail at the plant, so this was supposed to be a routine evidence-gathering mission.

Until Captain Morris got them lost again. Morris was in the lead Toyota with his DEA counterpart, another somewhat shifty looking guy who went by "Roberto." Two grunts were in the front. They weren't from Lt. Moring's team, so she really didn't know them that well, just that the guy was from Brooklyn and the butchy looking chick was from Atlanta, or somewhere close to it. Moring was fuming again. "If that worthless Morris was looking at his map instead of looking at Roberto's pictures of his whores, he *might* have noticed the sun is in our eyes instead of on our shoulders. That's assuming he chose not to look at a damned compass. Hey, Tom!"

"Yes, ma'am?"

"Whoa, amigo," Vasquez interrupted. "You can call the LT Alex, A.J., LT, or sir. Unless you want to get your head dented, do NOT call her ma'am. Clear?"

"Crystal. Yes, A.J.?"

"Tom, I say we're about fifteen clicks west of where we should be. What kind of territory are we in?"

"Bad territory, A.J. Since Pablo Escobar got taken down, this area has a turf war going on. It's like the range wars out west. No real leadership. They all shoot first and ask questions later."

"Out-fucking-standing. Okay, lock and load, gentlemen, and put your Kevlar on. Vasquez! See if you can get Captain Crunch's attention with the headlights. I've got to convince him he has us headed for a cluster."

"Yessir, LT," Vasquez replied while he pulled the bolt back on his M-16 and zipped up his body armor. The Lt. even had them hang vests on the interior of the doors. She believed in using any possible advantage. Her team liked that. Vasquez rolled down his window and waved as he flashed the headlights. It was noon local time, but in the near canopy of the Colombian highland forests, the flashing headlights should have easily been visible to anyone occasionally looking in the rearview mirror.

He and Moring both saw the flash and the small smoke trail as the RPG left the cover of the tree line headed toward the lead Toyota.

"Shit, I knew this was gonna happen."

BOOM!

The lead Toyota erupted in flame as the RPG made a direct hit in the front of the lead vehicle.

"Go…go…go. Everybody out of the vehicle. We're sitting ducks. Dink, you and Tom pull out everything you can carry, hit the woods on the right side, and wait. Get up on the comm and tell Searchlight we're taking fire. Vasquez, come with me. If there's anybody left up there, we have to get them." A.J. tore out of the Toyota at a dead run, Vasquez slightly behind her. Small arms fire was popping in their general direction, light submachine gun fire. A.J. saw the two back doors of the Land Cruiser open, and Morris and Roberto exited the truck, running from danger.

"Captain, you've got Marines in the truck. Are they all right?" Morris just stared at her. His eyes were blank, he was bleeding from a small cut on his forehead, and he looked like he had burns on one arm. "Captain. Your men. Goddammit – answer me!" She backhanded him. "Vasquez, check the truck. Roberto, think you could bother to shoot at them every now and then and help me get this useless piece of shit into the woods?"

Vasquez came running back to them, firing over his shoulder. “They’re gone, LT. We can’t help them. We can’t leave them either.”

“There’s not enough of us, Vasquez. We’ll have to come back. We need to get into the woods. We can return some fire, slow them down, then we E and E and call for a pickup. I don’t have a warm and fuzzy about the radios. I think these pricks may be listening. No telling whose side they’re on.”

“Roger that, LT.” He and Roberto helped drag Morris into the woods. A.J. located Tom and Dink pretty fast. “Did you guys grab the M40?”

“Roger that, LT.” He handed her a fiberglass rifle case.

“Okay, all of you head northwest. About five clicks there’s a ridgeline. Vasquez, you’re in charge. Get everybody out of here, and don’t stop. Got it?”

“What’re you gonna do, LT?”

“I’m gonna slow them down with my little friend.” She grinned, patting the sniper rifle.

“A.J., you can’t do this alone.”

“Move out, Vasquez, that’s an order. Besides, I’m gonna shoot and scoot. I can move faster without you guys. All I wanna do is wound a bunch of ’em and shoot out some tires. If I kill one, the rest will walk right by the bodies. If I wound one, it takes two to help. Now get the fuck outa Dodge!”

“Bitch!”

“Prick!”

Vasquez grinned, high-fived her, and turned away. He gathered up the rest and headed off northwest. They hadn’t gone fifty feet when he heard the M40 bark. *Another one bites the dust!*

CHAPTER 2

Ten minutes later, Vasquez and the others had traveled about a click to the northwest, headed into gradually rising terrain. He could hear occasional cracks from A.J.'s sniper rifle and dwindling fire from the automatic weapons. Two times he had definitely heard heavy machine gun fire, probably a fifty; but as soon as it had opened up, it had ceased. One RPG had detonated, but he could still hear A.J. shooting. It was always two or three minutes between rounds. *She knows what she's doing; they aren't having a good day* Then the shit started.

"Vasquez, exactly what in the hell do you think you're doing?" Morris asked, finally breaking his silence.

"Evading and escaping right now, Captain."

"By whose orders, Sergeant?"

"The LT's, Captain. She said head northwest a couple clicks and she'd catch up."

"Did she now? How fucking sweet of her! Do you see these bars on my shoulder, Sergeant? At what point were you going to ask me what my orders were?"

"When you started acting like a Marine officer, Captain. You haven't said a word since the RPG hit your truck while we were going down a road we had no business on. After that RPG killed two of our own. Remember all that, Captain? If we'd waited for you to start issuing orders, we'd all be dead by now. The LT did what she had to do. She's back there covering for us right now, but if you've got your head out of your ass and you're ready to start being a captain, take over. Sir."

"You insubordinate bastard. I'll have you and your precious LT up on charges as soon as we get back. Get me a map. We'll call for a helo pickup right now."

"That's not a good idea, sir. The LT said to get farther away, and she's not too sure the cowboys aren't listening to our PRCs. Besides—."

"I don't give a shit what that butch bitch said. Get me the radio!"

Vasquez did as he was told. It was too late to argue; he was at the point of obeying him or shooting him. The decision didn't have to be made right this instant thankfully. "Yes, sir, here you go. You might want to determine our coordinates prior to requesting that pickup, sir." He handed the map to the captain. Miller snatched the map out of Vasquez's hand and stared at it. He was biting his tongue to keep from laughing out loud; the captain may as well have been looking at sheet music for an opera. He was totally lost looking at the map.

"Sergeant, could you pick some coordinates for a pickup?"

Vasquez pointed to a spot on the map. “Here would be a pretty good spot, I think. We need to recon it and see if it can be secured with the resources we have.”

“I concur, so the coordinates would be…?”

“You mean the captain can’t determine that? Maybe we should wait for the lieutenant then.”

The captain’s eyes were shooting flames at Vasquez. “Are you trying to show contempt for a superior officer, Sergeant?”

“No, sir, to quote a movie I saw once, I’m doing my best to conceal my contempt.”

“I’ll handle it, Vasquez. And I’ll handle you and Moring when we get back.”

“I’ll be fuckin’ glad if that happens, captain.”

“You’re crazy, Vasquez. You’ll be glad about a court martial?”

“Absolutely, sir. You see, to be court martialed means I’ll be alive. If you’re running the show, nobody will be court martialed because we’ll be rotting here in the fucking jungle after the cowboys have killed us and cut off our heads for trophies.”

Stares were exchanged, and the captain blinked first. He turned and walked away, squeezing the map hard enough to make the ink start dripping.

Lt. Moring’s plan was going fairly well, but she was beginning to run low on ammunition. She had taken out two trucks with a shot to the radiator on one and a tire on the other. She was actually quite proud of the tire shot. She had deliberately shot out the tire right after the round had transited a cowboy’s leg, shattering the tibia on the way to the tire.

Shoot, move, shoot, move. A.J. slowly withdrew, firing a round and then retreating fifty meters. Sometimes to the rear, sometimes to one side or the other, but generally withdrawing, trying to inflict the maximum amount of pain on the cocaine cowboys. For the most part, she concentrated on wounding the bad guys. She aimed for a hand, a knee, something to make them scream for their mommas. As near as she could tell, there seemed to be about twenty of them. A third truck had arrived to join them. It had a fifty-caliber machine gun mounted in the back. A.J. knew it was a serious danger, both to her and their hopes of extraction. The first time one of the cowboys opened up, spraying half-inch diameter rounds where she had fired from five minutes ago, she had put a 7.62 round through his knee. When another cowboy replaced him, she put a round an inch above his nose. No one else got in the back of the truck.

She counted her remaining ammunition – six rounds; still way too many Colombians. She decided on a different strategy. A.J. carefully withdrew fifty meters and then began moving as fast as she could, looking for her unit's path. She would stop every three to five minutes to listen. The cowboys were still moving, but on foot now. She could hear them talking, but the distance prevented her being able to make out what was being said. She was fluent in Spanish, or at least the variant practiced here. She was especially good at the slang and cursing.

She located her team's trail after fifteen minutes of searching. "Jesus H. Fucking Christ," she muttered under her breath. "Stevie Wonder could trail you guys!" But what did she really expect? Aside from Marino and Vasquez, as far as she knew all the others were either desk jockeys or accustomed to working in the urban areas. She was worried. She had hoped the cowboys would leave. They weren't. She decided to loop back on the cowboys and hit them again; something had to be done to slow them down.

The terrain here was hilly. The vegetation was not a jungle, the altitude prevented that, but the woods were thick. The good news was there didn't seem to be any roads in the ridges where A.J. had sent her unit. The cowboys were pursuing, but had fanned out in a nearly 150-meter-wide front. A.J was concerned they would eventually find the trail left by her fellow Marines and the DEA agents. They were leaving tracks and broken brush five feet wide. They should have been traveling single file. She had even found water bottles and could smell the urine left where they had made a rest stop. Vasquez would have never allowed something so obvious. *It had to be Capt. Morris.*

She mentally cursed Morris as she looped back toward the cowboys. She watched them closely for a good fifteen minutes as they carefully eased up the ridge. While she watched, she reached into her fatigue pants pocket. She pulled out an old, smudged Zippo. It was a gift from her mother. A.J. didn't usually smoke. She remembered looking at Samantha with a quizzical look. "First time you have to shoot someone, pull it out. Rub it. It'll help. Keep it as a good luck charm." Her mother was right; somehow it did help.

One guy seemed to be in charge. He was wearing a big cowboy hat. She decided with her limited ammo the best move might be to take him out, wound a few more, and scoot again. She looked through the scope, trailing him as he walked. He was occasionally shouting an order. He gestured to a cowboy and stood waiting as a PRC-119 radio was brought to him. She was shocked! *It's just like our shit. No wonder they seem to know all our moves!*

A.J. watched his lips move, but at the 250-meter distance, she couldn't hear him. As she watched through the scope, the man looked directly at her. Had he seen her? Maybe a flash of sunlight reflected off the optics of the scope? No matter now. He was standing still, time for the shot. Her breathing slowed; nothing else existed. In her mind, she could literally see the round's course from the chamber, down the barrel, through 250 meters of mountain air, and into his forehead just above the eye. Time slowed to a crawl as her finger slowly closed on the trigger. It was a slight surprise when the rifle jumped slightly and spit the 175-grain projectile out the barrel. She immediately traversed to the next target; there was no need to look at the boss cowboy. A.J. knew he was dead before he hit the ground.

She had selected one of the point men who had seemed to know what he was looking at on the ground and in the underbrush. Several seconds later another projectile went through his knee. Nine mm bullets zinged in her general direction. She took off running to the south, charging like a bull for about two hundred meters and then gradually, quietly, turning back toward her unit's trail. She should have bought some time and hopefully would have the cowboys heading in the wrong direction for a while. It had been almost two hours since the first RPG hit the lead Toyota. Morris would screw everything up again unless she could catch them quickly.

CHAPTER 3

Vasquez and Moreno sat on a log as Captain Morris spoke to Searchlight on the PRC-119. He was requesting an immediate pickup via helo. Apparently he had managed to figure out the coordinates. Vasquez listened as Morris asked for a pickup for five. He had forgotten the LT. When questioned by Searchlight, the captain had re-grouped, explaining there were two KIA and that the lieutenant was missing. Morris really started stuttering when asked why they were so far from their intended location; he gave no logical explanation.

What Vasquez saw as the most damaging tidbit of bullshit dispensed by the captain was his assertion to Searchlight that the LZ was secure. Vasquez had just turned to Moreno and whispered, "B.S." when Morris turned toward them. "Got something to say, Sergeant?"

"Not really, sir, I think you covered most of it."

"Most of it, Vasquez?"

"Yes, sir, I mean other than bullshitting them about being lost, ignoring our dead, forgetting the LT, and telling them the LZ was secure when we haven't even reconned it, you were outstanding. Topnotch, sir."

"We'll settle this when we get back to base, Sergeant. I still fail to see how you can put so much trust in a twenty-one-year-old first lieutenant in S-2."

"Maybe because she's brilliant, she outshoots everyone on the range every time we qualify, and maybe because she has bigger cajones than most men. Her dad was a recon gunny sergeant in 'Nam. She knows her shit, sir. You would've done better to listen to her. Do you intend to just leave her here?"

"No, I expect she'll show when she's done hiding."

Vasquez laughed aloud. "Hiding my ass, Captain. You haven't heard the shooting I guess. She's the only reason the cowboys haven't caught up with us yet."

Tom, the DEA agent, had been quiet until now, but he couldn't stand it any longer. "Morris, I'm not a Marine, I'm not in charge of your men, but I'll remind you, you're working for us. The DEA is running the show here. You're support. I've listened to your shit for two hours. Do what you want with your people, but rest assured, I'll be filing a report too. You aren't going to look good in it. How long until the helo gets here?"

A much more reserved Morris replied, "About thirty minutes."

"How far are we from the LZ?"

"About a kilometer."

"You better hope the LT shows up. Otherwise, we wait for her."

"Yes, sir." Morris was seething. "Let's move out, if it's okay with Tom that is," he sneered.

A.J. hustled now, following the trail of her unit. She had to be getting close. Assuming she had been fairly successful leaving the cowboys behind, she hoped she was two clicks ahead of them. She looked at her watch; it had been two hours and twenty minutes since the shit hit the fan. The top of the ridge should be close. That would be where she hoped Vasquez would have taken them. *Talking, I hear talking, in English!* A.J. knew she was close. She paused again, trying to hear. That was when her relief turned to dismay. More voices, Spanish this time! There was no way! The cowboys should be behind her, way behind. These voices were coming from her left, to the west. It had to be another group of cowboys. *Fuck, they've called in reinforcements. There has to be a road down there somewhere!* Then she heard the rotors. It was faint, but unmistakable. It was a Huey. This was bad, very bad. Someone had called for an extraction without verifying the LZ was clear.

She was sprinting now. She needed to warn the helo! In a few moments she saw the group on the edge of a clearing. "Call the helo off, we have to abort! There's a second group of cowboys coming up the ridge out of the west. They're closing, give me the radio!" The Huey was close, banking into the wind to flare.

"Not happening, Lieutenant. We're leaving," Morris shouted.

"You stupid fuck! You've got two killed already today. Are you trying for more?" Vasquez handed her the PRC-119.

"I'll see you in prison, Marine!" Morris screamed.

"Tango two-two to helo, abort, abort. LZ is not secure. How copy?"

Before the helo could answer, small arms fire broke out to the west. A small smoke trail headed up for the helo. It was an RPG. At close range and in skilled hands, they could be deadly to a helicopter. Thank God the Colombians didn't know the Huey was out of range. Only an incredibly lucky shot would have a chance. The Huey banked hard, throttling up. The blades were popping hard as they bit air.

"Copy two-two, we're aborting. Thanks for the warning!"

Morris grabbed the mic. "This is Captain Morris. I'm ordering you to make the pickup, copy?"

"Oh, we copy, Morris, but we're not Marines. We're private contractors. We were told we had a secure LZ. My first responsibility is to my crew and aircraft. Order all you want. We're headed back to Cali."

Tom spoke quietly. "Morris, you're an embarrassment. A.J., what do we do now?"

"We need to hurt the new bunch of cowboys, Tom, and then we need to run like rabbits."

Suddenly the PRC-119 came to life. "Senorita, we are coming for you, senorita. You want to play with us? We can play. Then I will put all your heads on sticks. You last, senorita, after my men have some fun with you."

A.J. grabbed the mic. "What's wrong, Jose? You haven't had enough fun yet? Want me to shoot some more knees? Bring it on, cowboy!" Then she launched into Spanish with a tirade that included some very colorful metaphors. She grabbed the radio and shut it off. "Guess we can assume they can monitor our com." She grabbed the map and gazed at it for a full ten seconds. "Dink, Vasquez, we're going to the ridge to shoot some cowboys. The rest of you head east, down the ridge. Make all the noise you want. I want them to be able to follow us. Wait at the creek, we'll only be ten minutes or so. The three of them grabbed M-16s and headed up the slope, fanning out.

As the two DEA agents and Morris headed toward the creek, they heard the M-16s popping in several locations. Fifteen minutes later the group assembled at the creek. As she waded into the creek, A.J. told the others, "Follow me, guys. We'll head upstream a couple hundred meters. We've got to lose these assholes long enough to regroup and get picked up. We put a hurt on them, but we're all low on ammo. Tom, did you pull your sat-phone out of the Toyota?"

"Yeah, A.J., I've got it in my backpack."

"How long to set it up?"

"Never timed it, but five minutes? I don't know if we'll have an available satellite right now. We don't have 100 percent coverage. It's pretty new shit."

"Okay, soon as we can get a chance, call your people. Make sure it's someone you trust. I have a feeling some of people have been bought off; we know the military com is compromised. Call a friend, tell them the situation. We'll have to use the sat-phone or the next pickup won't go any better than this one." Tom nodded assent.

For the next hour, the entire team hustled along in total silence. They slogged up the creek about a thousand meters. When they left, A.J. had them exit on one side, making a mess of the bank and leaving trails into the woods. Then they returned to the creek another 200 meters, exiting carefully, stepping from rock to rock and staying single file. The light was beginning to fade; unless the Colombians had a dog or a really sharp tracker, they should have given them the slip. A.J. allowed one break long enough for Tom to set up his phone and call in their situation.

"Hey, A.J., my guys want to know if we're in a position to call back in an hour. They think they can put an extraction plan together by then."

"Tell them fine, we can wait. I could be wrong, but I think we're okay for now." Tom conveyed the message to his DEA people and signed off. "Hey, A.J., got any idea what airtime on this thing costs?"

"I'll pay it, Tom, put it on my tab, okay?"

"Sure thing, LT."

"Let's go, gentlemen, remember, single file and quiet. It's getting dark. I'm hoping they're backing off. I guess it depends on how pissed they are. Tom, do we even know who the fuck these people are?"

"We have ideas, but in this area, there's a couple possibilities."

"Any idea how persistent they're going to be?"

"Yes, and you won't like it. I think they've got something to prove. They want DEA out of here. You guys are collateral damage I'm afraid."

A.J. just nodded. "Let's go then."

An hour later, on top of a small ridge in a clearing, Tom set up his phone again and checked in. He asked for the map and A.J.'s best estimate of where they were. A couple of minutes later, he gave a set of coordinates to her and asked if they could be there by 2300 hours. It was about three clicks away. It would be tough in the dark, but doable. She nodded. They had already done ten or fifteen clicks today. Not far at all on flat ground, but pretty grueling in forest going almost straight up and down. The DEA guys and Morris were used to driving desks; they were looking rough. Dink, A.J., and Vasquez weren't breathing hard.

Tom terminated the call and turned to the group. "Here's the deal, guys, a friend called a friend. We've got a Plan A and Plan B. Plan A: the Air Force has some assets in the area on a training exercise. They're Special Ops out of Hurlburt Field in Florida. They're sending an AC-130 gunship for air support and a Pave Low MH-53 for extraction. The 130 can be on station by 2200. He can loiter in case we need help. The helo at 2300."

"What's Plan B?" A.J. asked.

"They're sending a reinforced Colombian Army convoy that'll be here at first light, but they're giving them coordinates a good five clicks away just in case there's an intelligence leak."

"So once we're at the LZ, there shouldn't be any friendlies there before daybreak, correct?"

"Roger that, LT."

"Okay then, we've got about three or so hours to do three clicks in the dark with nothing but a compass and a map. Sounds like fun, huh, Vasquez? Dink?"

"Piece 'a cake, LT."

"Okay then, let's go, should be an interesting evening." She turned and headed out.

CHAPTER 4

Alternate LZ

2130 hours

When A.J. arrived, she could see why the spot had been picked as an LZ. In the light from the half moon, she could see what appeared to be a couple of acres cleared in the forest nearly on the top of another ridge. Tom had said he thought the site was a coca field the DEA had sprayed with defoliant, and it looked as though he was absolutely correct.

Upon arriving, A.J., Dink, and Vasquez had done a quick check of the perimeter. The site looked and sounded clear, at least for the time being. "Dink, Vasquez, set up a perimeter about a hundred meters out and listen. Is that okay with you, Captain Morris?"

"Would it really matter, Lieutenant? You seem to have assumed operational command here."

"No, you're right. It probably wouldn't matter if you agreed or not, sir. Just thought I'd ask." Obviously the captain was furious. So be it. "Tom, let's discuss how we're going to communicate with the pickup team. I hope the cowboys are far enough behind us that it doesn't matter, but we have to assume they're listening to our comm."

"I know, I told my guy that. The 130 is going to come up on button four. Soon as we reply, they'll switch to button seven. We'll all go up three buttons every conversation. Anything gets screwed up, we go to button two-two. They'll call first. They'll be using Ghost one-niner as a call sign. We'll still be Tango two-two."

"Okay, works for me." The group seemed to have taken up sides; Tom and A.J. were sitting on one log while Captain Morris and Roberto were seated about twenty feet away. Conversations were between the pairs and muted. As far as A.J. was concerned, the less she had to say to Morris the better. She looked up at him and Roberto in time to see Roberto cutting the end off a fat cigar. She walked over to him.

"I hope you're planning on eating that thing."

"No, Lieutenant, I intend to smoke it."

"Like hell you will. We don't need the light or the smell, not this close to the finish line."

"I'm afraid you can't tell me what to do, senorita. I'm not one of your boys."

"I can tell you what do, Roberto. If you'll recall, you work for me," Tom said in a low voice. "Eat it or chunk it. If she says no smoking, it's no smoking."

Roberto put the cigar back in his pocket and chuckled. "Okay, boss, for now." He shrugged and turned away, revealing a tattoo of a scorpion on his neck.

A.J. saw a look of surprise on Morris's face. Apparently he thought, as did Moring, that Roberto was the DEA team leader. It seemed there was a relationship between him and Tom that A.J. and her team, including Morris, was unaware of.

The confrontation was behind them for now. A.J. walked back to her log and checked the volume on the PRC 119. It was on low and set to button four. As she sat, she thought she could hear a low droning noise. She stood and walked a few meters out into the coca field and listened intently. Yes, it was there, a low but unmistakable drone. The 130 had arrived it seemed. She was quite familiar with the AC-130 Spectre. The Spectre was basically an airborne battleship. Initially developed during the Vietnam conflict, it had evolved from a Lockheed C-130. Originally fitted with mini Gatling guns and used for ground support, in had been advanced over the years and now held two 20 mm Vulcan cannons, a Bofors 40 mm autocannon, and a single 105 mm cannon. It was equipped with low-light sensors and could deliver unbelievable amounts of firepower with high precision. They were Air Force Special Operations aircraft but could be called on to support any ground operations requiring their unique capabilities.

Suddenly there was a hiss and pop on the PRC, followed by, "Tango two-two, Ghost one-niner, how copy, over?"

A.J. ran to the radio and answered, "Ghost one-niner, Tango two-two copies Lima-Charlie over."

She quickly switched to button seven.

"Two–two, we're on station. We believe we have a heat signature at planned extraction LZ. Any way you can confirm with a visual signal?"

"Give us a minute, one-niner." *Shit, we don't even have a freakin' flashlight.* Then an idea came to her. She ran to Dink's camera equipment. Thank God he had thought to snatch it when he exited the Toyota. It really shouldn't have been a surprise. She didn't think he even went to the head without his camera gear. There it was, the strobe. She went to the radio, advanced it to button ten, and called up, "Ghost one-niner, visual coming up. All we have is a camera strobe. We don't have IR." She ran back into the coca field, listened until she thought she had the general direction of the 130, and popped the flash three times as fast as the capacitor would recharge.

"Okay two-two, we have you, is the LZ secure, and do you have any friendlies in the area?"

"No, we have a ground force due at first light."

"Then you have company. Make sure you hold your position; if they get any closer, we're going to go to weapons release."

Why are these cowboys so intent on killing us? A.J. was puzzled. It just didn't add up. And how did they know where they were so quickly? Something was very wrong, and she wanted to know…

BRRRRRAAAP. There was a sudden earth-shattering noise. To A.J. it sounded like the heavens had opened up with an enormous fart. The impacts of the thousands of 20-mm shells could be felt both through her feet and behind her belt buckle.

It was a truly impressive demonstration of firepower. Just a few minutes later, flashes of light popped out of the sky again, followed a few seconds later by the faint report of the cannon on the 130 firing and the explosions of the rounds hitting something on the ground. The resulting small explosions seemed to be a kilometer or so away to the east. *Jesus they're coming at us from both sides of the ridge. We were dead meat without the Air Force!*

"Ghost one-niner, Tango two-two, your ride is inbound at this time, be ready for extraction. Contact Reacher one nine on final button. Copy?"

"Copy one-niner, thanks for your help, Tango two-two out." She switched to button two-two on the PRC and pressed the push-to-talk button. "Reacher one-nine, Tango two-two, how copy?"

"Two-two, copy. We're sixty seconds out, have your people ready. Can you confirm number for pickup?"

"Reacher we have six, copy?"

"Copy two-two, advise your team to haul ass to the ramp as soon as we're down. We have LZ in sight two-two."

How the hell can they have the LZ in sight? Then, just as she remembered the crew was likely wearing night vision goggles, the whole team heard and felt the helo suddenly pass over. All A.J. could *see* was something darker than the night sky as the hulking helicopter passed over at about twenty meters, just above the treetops. Hearing and feeling, however, were altogether different. The vibrations from the fat blades could be felt in the pit of her stomach. The sound of the turbines driving the blades was nearly obscured by the popping of the blades. She had been around '53s before. They were always impressive, and the Pave Low was a CH-53 on steroids. She knew the skinny on the Pave Low. It was designed for long range, low-altitude penetration to either drop off or extract people from behind enemy lines. The helo was heavily armed and had full night vision and advanced navigation capabilities to get in and out. It also was equipped with titanium armor in critical areas.

"Dink, Vasquez, load up!" she yelled, waiting for an answer before beginning to collect their gear. The Pave Low flared and set down about seventy-five meters away from the edge of the woods in the approximate middle of the coca field. The entire group took off running toward the helo. It sat with its ramp down in the rear, rotors feathered, and turbines sounding like they were at full throttle. The interior of the bird was bathed in red light. There were two pararescuemen in full Kevlar on the ramp. Armed with M-16s with grenade launchers mounted under the barrels, they were beckoning the group to hurry.

As she approached the helo, A.J. noticed the AC-130 hurling another bolt of lightning out of the sky; at least it looked like a bolt of lightning. It was a hell of a lot of lead; she knew that.

A.J. and Morris boarded the bird last, running up the ramp into the red-lit interior just in front of the two pararescuemen. She took a seat in a canvas-slung side-mounted seat as the rescue men signaled the crew chief everyone was aboard; and before she could even fasten her belt, the huge chopper lifted off.

After a few fairly violent gyrations, the Pave Low began to assume a more normal flight path, gaining altitude and heading in what seemed like a more or less northern direction, toward Cali. The seating in the chopper seemed to echo the division of the unit; A.J., Tom, Dink, and Vasquez on one side, Roberto and Morris on the other.

A.J. watched Morris stand and head to the crew chief, tilting his head toward him to be heard over the background noise of the helo. The crew chief brought the captain a headset, and Morris seemed to initiate an animated conversation.

Tom leaned to A.J.'s ear. "Doesn't look good, Lieutenant. It looks to me like Morris is setting you up for trouble."

"Yeah, LT, you're being thrown under the bus for sure." Vasquez's voice exuded anger.

"I can deal with shits like Morris." A.J. was fuming. Someone was going to pay, one way or another. "I'll figure it out. It pisses me off to have to cover my ass when I know I was right, but I can do it. Don't worry, I got this."

Two hours later, at 0200 hours, the helo landed in Cali. A.J. was a little surprised that the helo was still spooled up as they exited. She turned to the crew chief to shake his hand. "Thanks for the ride. We were screwed for sure without you guys. If you're going to be here tomorrow, my guys and I would love to buy the crew a drink, maybe a lot of drinks."

"You're welcome, Lieutenant. We'd take you up on the offer, but we've never been to Colombia, still haven't. We were never here tonight. In fact, we have to leave before sunup, or we turn into a pumpkin. Good luck, Lieutenant, you're a good soldier. Someone is trying to screw you. Something else you need to know. The electronic warfare officer on the Spectre told me something on a private com; someone in your group was wearing a homing device. Someone wanted to know where you were. Your unit was set up; I doubt you're supposed to be alive right now. You need to watch your back. See you again." He slapped A.J. on the ass and ran back up the ramp.

That explains a lot, that's how they knew where we were all the time. She turned away from the rotor wash and walked toward the group gathered on the ramp. Her major waved her over. "Lieutenant, we have a serious problem.

Captain Morris wants to have you brought up on charges. I need your after-action report in my hands within an hour after we get back to the hotel. Don't discuss this with anyone. I want all of you taking separate cabs back to the hotel. Remember Moring, an hour!"

A.J. sat in silence. Her mind whirled as she rode through the mostly dark streets of Cali to the non-descript hotel the DEA had commandeered four blocks off the business district. Ostensibly it was a real hotel and actually did take customers. It had the normal features of a hotel. By the time she exited the cab she had formulated a plan. When she walked through the lobby, she was thankful to see Hector at the desk. Hector was sweet on A.J., she was sure of it. She leaned up to him and asked, "Hector, I need some food brought up to my room in thirty minutes, and I need you to bring it. Will you do that for me?"

"Sí, Senorita Moring, anything for you, you know that."

"Buena, Hector."

Her room was on the second floor, and she ran up the stairs rather than waiting for the elevator. As soon as she got to the room, she stripped off her clothes and booted the laptop her brother had set up for her. It made it much easier to type her after action reports and anything else through Word Perfect on her printer.

She ran through a shower and back to her computer in very non-regulation camo bikini panties and a tank top. The water supply in Cali was questionable in both quantity and quality. Thankfully she'd accomplished her shower. Fifteen minutes later, she was done with her report. Now it was time for her CYA. She inserted a floppy drive into the computer and set it to copy her after action reports for the last thirty days. While it churned, she quickly handwrote a letter explaining her situation and addressed a manila envelope to a Linda Kowalski in Arlington, Virginia.

She dressed quickly. No need to tease Hector any more than necessary. Once her computer indicated the files were written to the floppy, she dropped it and the note in the envelope. Hector showed up right on time with a bowl of soup and a loaf of bread. She took it and hugged him, whispering in his ear, “Hector, I need this letter to get to the States as soon as possible, and not through the hotel mail system, *comprende*? It’s very important to me.”

Hector nodded. “I can do it, Senorita Moring. My cousin works with the airline; she can have this mailed in Miami by noon today, right after she lands. Consider it done.”

A.J. handed Hector a fifty and kissed him on the cheek. “Thank you for the food, Hector. I was starved,” she announced in a much louder tone. She hoped this worked; she was going to need something to go right. Her little dot matrix printer chugged away while she worked on the soup and bread. She hadn’t eaten since breakfast and hadn’t realized how hungry she’d been until she smelled the food.

A look at her watch indicated her time was up. Time to face the music, or, in this case, the major. She grabbed the report and headed to the elevator. The major had a two-room suite on the top floor. Minutes later she was knocking on his door.

“Come!”

She opened the door and walked to his desk. She handed him the report and stood at parade rest. “Sir, our KIA, we need to recover the bodies, sir.”

The major held his hand up in a “stop” gesture while he read each page of her report. “Please take a seat, Moring.” He was still reading. As the major read the last page, he stood and walked to the open window. He pulled a cigar out of his pocket and lit it. Obviously he was thinking. "Lieutenant Moring, this is a really fucked-up mess. I hope you realize that. I'm glad your first concern is the two young Marines who gave their lives. The Colombians have recovered the bodies; they'll be back in Cali today. I have to ask you, Moring, did you really slap Morris?"

"Yes, sir, I did. He had just gotten out of a vehicle that had been hit by an RPG; he seemed to be in shock. We were taking fire, and I was trying to make him snap out of it."

"He claims you slapped him, insulted him, and took command of his unit. He wants you charged with conduct unbecoming an officer. That's serious. I, on the other hand, have got two dead and have to explain why the *fucking* Air Force had to come in and pick up my Marines."

"Well, Major, that's what *fucking* happened, sir."

The major stared at her for a full minute. "Lieutenant, I really don't give a shit about the captain's bruised ego. What I do care about is this making me look bad. I can probably get him to go away if you'll revise your report. You never slapped him, his car hit a mine killing the two marines, and the Colombian Army brought you guys in."

A.J. shook her head. "Sorry, Major, I won't do it."

The major looked at her and blew cigar smoke in her face. "It's always black and white to your kind, isn't it, Lieutenant?" He picked up his phone and dialed two numbers. "Do it," he growled. "Have it your way, Moring. Consider yourself under arrest until I can convene an Article 32 hearing. You'll be escort be back to your room. You're confined to quarters until the hearing. Dismissed."

First Lieutenant A.J. Moring saluted, turned, and left the office to be met by two security guards. As she walked to the elevator between them, she thought she had had better days. She really hoped the envelope got to Linda. Somebody was going to get his or her ass kicked, and Moring would be happy to do it personally. *T.D. would forgive me if he was here.*

CHAPTER 5

Alexandria, Virginia

1100 hrs.

Thomas Hendrix was enjoying retirement. He had handed the reins over to Tony King with no regrets. Well, almost no regrets. Tony would do a great job; Hendrix had hit sixty-five and was ready. Actually, it was his longtime partner, Linda, who had finally shoved him off the cliff to retirement. Linda worked for Tony now as an analyst and de-facto second-in-command as she had for Thomas. In two more years she would retire as well.

Since there was no longer a problem with being employed at the FBI, their long relationship no longer needed to be kept under wraps. As a result, Hendrix had spent the night at Linda's last night. He was up drinking coffee and working on his memoirs when there was some racket at the door. It was the mailman. Thomas watched as the mail dropped through the slot in the front door. He took a sip from his coffee, rose from the dining room table, and went to collect the mail. He knew Linda would like seeing it on her hall table rather than scattered on the floor.

A medium-sized manila envelope caught his eye. It was addressed to Linda, hand addressed at that, in bold, block letters. It was marked “Urgent” and had no return address; it was postmarked from Miami, Florida. Hendrix deliberated. Was it urgent enough for him to open it? Or would Linda be pissed at him? The debate was short-lived. He decided if a quick glance at the inside confirmed it was truly urgent, she would forgive him. She would probably forgive him regardless; therefore, it was important to verify the true urgency of the package. The contents were sparse, one sheet of paper and a computer floppy disc. As he read the letter, and especially the signature, a flood of memories and emotions washed through him. This letter was truly urgent. His hands shook slightly as he dialed Linda’s private number.

“Kowalski,” a familiar voice answered on the other end of the line.

“Hi, it’s me. I opened a piece of your mail; it was marked urgent. It’s from Alexandra, Sam and Steve’s daughter. She’s in trouble; she needs our help. Can we meet with Tony ASAP?”

“Of course, but he’s in Quantico this morning.”

“Even better, I’m throwing on some clothes. I’ll head that way. There’s a note and a computer floppy in the package, so see if we can get a meeting room with a computer and several big monitors.”

“Sure, what kind of trouble is she in? Where is she?”

“I don’t want to say on this line. We’ll discuss it in Quantico, okay?”

“Of course, dear, I’ll see you when you get there. I’ll leave D.C. immediately myself, as soon as I can let someone know to find Tony and have him ready for an emergency meeting. See you soon, lover!"

Thomas smiled as he said, "I love you too," and hung up. *What a strange relationship.* Almost twenty-five years and they could just now admit their true feelings for each other to their business associates, and even themselves. A very small number of people had figured it out many years ago, but they had maintained their silence. Even now that the two had gone public, as it were, Linda steadfastly refused to marry Thomas. She said it was out of respect for her deceased husband, but there had to be another reason. Hell, Hendrix and Linda hadn't even considered becoming "involved" until well after both of their spouses had been dead for years. Even then, it had begun as more of a convenience than an affair.

Hendricks shaved and dressed and grabbed the envelope as he headed out the door. They had a friend in trouble, and the cavalry would be coming to the rescue. The only thing missing were their old friends Samantha and Steve. And Kenny, of course. But A.J. had been adamant about not involving her parents until at least this preliminary round was over. She said something about fearing Sam and Steve might use the "nuclear option." Hendricks smiled. Alexandra had no idea how much she resembled her parents. He decided he would respect her wishes, for the time being anyway.

Forty-five minutes later, he walked into the lobby in Tony's building in Quantico. She was waiting for him. She hugged him and pinned a "Visitor" pass to his jacket.

"I called Tony when the guards told me you came through the gate. He's going to meet us in the secure conference room. Do we need anyone else?"

"I imagine we will, but I'll let Tony and you make that decision. I'm not running the show anymore, and I don't want anyone to be confused about who is."

A few moments later, Tony and Linda were reading A.J.'s handwritten note while Thomas loaded her floppy disc into the computer.

"Well," Tony opened, "it looks like A.J. was involved in an operation in Colombia that went very wrong. The rest of her team got out, but from her note, it appears she has a serious concern that she may wind up being used as a scapegoat for someone else's piss-poor performance. Is her last after-action report on the floppy?"

"Yes, in fact, it looks like that's all that is on here. I'm seeing every after action report for the last month. This looks like CYA material, but for what? Looks like she knows she's in trouble, but why? Her after-action report looks like she deserves a medal. I don't get it."

"Okay, let's do this. Linda, have somebody find her. All we have in this note is she's in Cali, Colombia, deployed with the DEA. We need to talk to her, and then we'll know what to do. Thomas, go ahead and print all her after-action reports then give the disc to the digital forensic team. I'll initiate the chain–of-custody paperwork. Strike that. Linda, this was addressed to you. Go ahead and start it. It'll have Thomas's prints on it, but we can establish what computer it came from and when it was encoded. I have a feeling we'll need that. Let's get back together in an hour or so and see what we know."

CHAPTER 6

Guantanamo Bay, Cuba

Lt. Moring thought her new home was the nicest jail cell she had ever seen. It was almost identical to a motel room, except it had no windows, no phone, and definitely no minibar.

After her discussion with Major Lewis back in Cali, two members of the security detail had escorted her to her room. As she had halfway expected, the room had been tossed. Her computer was gone, and anything that had been in a drawer was pretty much on the floor. “I want it noted my quarters have been trashed and my laptop is missing,” she’d told a guard.

“So noted,” he answered in a bored voice. A.J. made a point of writing down both of their names. She looked for her camera to get some evidence, and of course found it missing as well. *Well, I’ll either* see *it again or I won’t. Not really anything I can do about it now.*

"Lieutenant, you need to gather up your gear. We're escorting you to Gitmo in about three hours. You're confined to quarters; one of us will be outside at all times. Do you want some breakfast?"

A.J. was staring out the window. The sun was coming up over the city. It was actually quite pretty. *I hope the Pave Low helo didn't turn into a pumpkin.* "Yes, that would be great. I'll pack while I'm waiting."

Once the security guards had left the room, she locked the door and dug, looking for her Sony Walkman. Her brother had designed and built it for her. It looked like a Walkman and actually played. Inside were enough memory chips to load all the files on her laptop's twenty-megabyte memory other than the DOS operating system and the few programs she had on it. It was there! Even if the floppy she sent Linda got lost or confiscated, she still had her laptop's data living in the Walkman. She packed her few belongings. One dress uniform, four sets of BDUs, shoes, underwear, and a few toiletries. It easily fit in her gunnysack.

A knock on the door announced breakfast. She sat on her bed watching a Spanish language station while she ate. Spanish had come easily for some reason. After a while it had seemed a more logical system of speech than English, and swearing in Spanish just sounded so obscene and romantic at the same time. She just *loved* cursing in Spanish!

A ride in a dirty, black Suburban and two aircraft later, she was in Cuba. She had been sitting in her cozy cell in the basement of the BOQ eating a pretty decent dinner when there was a knock on the door.

"It's open," she replied. A twenty-something young lady in a set of BDUs with captain's bars on her shoulders entered. She was short, brunette, and reasonably attractive. She took in her surroundings and walked over to stand by the bed. A.J. stood and saluted as she had been trained.

"Lieutenant Moring, my name is Captain Jernigan. I've been appointed by the JAG office at Gitmo to represent you in your Article 32 hearing. At this point, I don't know a damned thing about your case. This is a meeting so I can familiarize you with how your hearing will be conducted and to answer any questions you might have. Then we can discuss how we'll proceed with your defense. There's no need for formality in here; if you wish, you can call me Amanda." She offered her hand.

A.J. shook her hand and sat back down on the bed. "Okay, Amanda, if that's how it's going to be, you can call me A.J. or LT. That's what I'm accustomed to. Do you mind if I eat while you talk? This is only my second meal in about two days."

"That's fine. Are you familiar with an Article 32?"

"More or less, it's a preliminary hearing to determine if the Corps will proceed with a full-fledged court martial."

"That's correct. It's a lot like a civilian grand jury hearing. It has some advantages and some disadvantages for the defendant. On the plus side, you'll have an opportunity to present a defense, your side of the story. On the other hand, the case will be heard by a general officer, not a group of citizens. The general officer will have sole discretion about the outcome. Any questions so far?"

"Yeah, several. First, you don't look any older than me. You say you're with the JAG office, so I'm assuming you're a lawyer. Where did you go to law school and how many cases like this have you had?"

"Vanderbilt, and you'll be my second case."

"Well, good start, I'm a Vandy grad too. How did your first hearing go?"

"I lost."

"Out-fucking-standing."

"Look, Lieutenant, I can understand your concerns, but…"

"Look, let's do this. Get familiar with my case. Review the charges, look at my jacket. Interview the men in my squad, and we'll talk again. Sound good? Oh, and I want my computer back. My quarters in Cali were tossed. I'm sure the official term was searched, but my laptop was taken, and I want it back."

"Okay, Lt. Moring, I'll look into that."

"You do that, Capt. Jernigan. By the way, from what you've been told, what am I charged with?"

"Striking a fellow officer and conduct unbecoming."

"Okay, just curious." A.J. stood and saluted. Jernigan returned her salute and walked to the door.

"Guard! I'm done here." She turned to A.J. "I'll be back, Lieutenant."

A.J. nodded and went back to her dinner. A shower and a nap sounded good right now.

Quantico, Virginia

Linda, Hendrix, and Tony were seated again in the secure conference room. With them was Evan Wilson, an analyst Tony had come to value for his extensive ability to work inside and outside the system of the United States military establishment.

"Here's what we know," Tony began, "Alexandra Moring is currently being confined to quarters in Gitmo.

That information in itself was a bit of a struggle for Evan to determine. She's being charged with conduct unbecoming a Marine Corps officer as well as physically assaulting a fellow officer. We've reviewed her after-action report and were able to obtain an after-action report filed by her superiors. There's almost no resemblance between the two. We know she's been assigned a JAG defense attorney, but, and this is a biggie, her entire unit and the Tom character with the DEA have disappeared. They're completely off the grid. Also, according to Evan, the Air Force assets Alexandra describes have officially not been anywhere near Colombia in months. There's either someone in a high place covering up a pile of shit, or Alexandra is totally crazy."

Linda looked hard at Tony. "Boss, I'm sorry, but I've known this young lady since she was born. Number one, never call her Alexandra. Don't ask, it's complicated. Number two, she is probably incapable of lying, and she's not crazy. Eccentric, unusual? Sure. Crazy? Hell no."

"I agree. I think it's critical we find these people. People can cover up shit, but they can't hide the smell. This didn't happen twenty-five years ago. I'm sure Evan is good, but I know people at DEA, and I have friends that have friends at Hurlburt. That's where the Air Force assets A.J. mentioned had to have come from. Have Evan work on where the guys from her unit are. I'll cover the other two pieces of the puzzle. Someone is trying to bury A.J., but I suspect it's more a matter of covering up some screw-up more than an issue with Moring."

"Okay, Thomas, I agree. What about Steve and Samantha? Where are they on this?"

"A.J. made it clear in her note she doesn't want them involved," Linda answered.

“But why? I don’t get that.”

“You don’t know A.J. You think Sam and Steve are hard-headed? A.J. inherited that in spades from them. There’s a reason that only she knows. For now, there’s nothing to be gained by telling them.”

Hendrix chimed in at this point, “We all have more information to gather. Has anyone spoken to her JAG attorney?”

Tony shook his head. “Not yet. But I’ll be talking to her soon. Do you guys think we should send someone?”

“I think I should go.” Thomas spoke quietly. “It’s not time to leave yet. I’d like to personally carry A.J.’s after-action report, along with the report your forensic guys come up with. I also need to find the rest of her team. Or, rather, we need to find them. I don’t know yet what line of crap is being presented as far as what A.J. is supposed to have done. We need to nail down what she really did. That’s her defense. Whatever the charges, the truth will be her defense.”

CHAPTER 7

Guantanamo Bay, Cuba

A.J. sat in a chair; Captain Jernigan sat across from her in the room that the United States Marine Corps had decided to use for the lieutenant's quarters/cell she was confined to pending her Article 32 hearing. A small stack of files sat on the table between the two women.

"Well, A.J., at least we now have a pretty good idea what we're up against. As required by the U.S. Code of Military Justice, I have the full description of your charges. The prosecution isn't required to submit how they intend to prove their case at this point, just what they are asking you to be charged with."

"And?"

"The list isn't too long, but it's not pretty. Captain Morris wants you charged with striking a fellow officer and conduct unbecoming, specifically commandeering the unit thereby usurping his command as a superior officer. Then, Major Lewis also wants to charge you with disobeying a direct order by failing to submit an after-action report after being specifically ordered to do so and with conduct unbecoming an officer by being verbally disrespectful after he informed you of your failure to submit the report. Are you going to deny all of this?"

"Amanda, first, do you have my computer? And have you talked to any of the rest of my unit, or Tom with the DEA?"

"No, no, and no. Your computer has disappeared; every single member of your unit is unavailable due to national security and mission requirements, and the DEA in Cali denies having a Tom working for them. Between the stonewall I keep hitting and my client not telling me a damned thing, my head should have bruises from impacting a brick wall repeatedly. You've got to give me something, A.J. The Article 32 *will* happen. I can delay it *some* since we can't get rebuttal witnesses or statements, but it's going to happen within three or four days. You can't hold out on me forever!"

"Captain, it's been seventy-two hours since all this went down. I don't know you. Right now, I'm essentially being held in solitary confinement. I'm unable to contact anyone I know or believe to be trustworthy. The people who could act as witnesses to what actually happened have disappeared." A.J. looked at her watch. "Captain Jernigan, it's 0900 hours. Please go back to your JAG office. Stay near a phone and please find me a laptop and a printer, even if you have to bring it to me and take it with you when you leave. You should be getting a phone call very soon. After you get that call, come see me and we'll talk.

I'm sorry, but right now, this is how it has to be." A.J. stood and saluted Jernigan. The captain stood and returned her salute then attempted to hug A.J.

"I'll do as you ask. Is there anyone I can call for you? Just to let them know you're all right?" She backed away, "I'm sorry, A.J. I think I invaded your space. I apologize. I didn't mean…"

"No, Amanda, no apology needed. I'm just not wired for that, at least not now. It's me. You didn't do anything wrong. Please just go. Wait for the call, and then we can talk."

Amanda returned to her office completely puzzled. Her defense of Lt. Moring had seemed simple when assigned to her. The more she looked into it, the more puzzling it became. A.J.'s attitude and demeanor were something she was not accustomed to. The young lieutenant's body had become as stiff as a board when Jernigan had attempted to hug her. Then there was the amount of roadblocks being placed in her path by the Corps. It was becoming suspicious. Moring wouldn't say it, but it was becoming obvious to anyone with eyes there was a cover-up underway. Jernigan couldn't blame Moring for being suspicious.

The young lieutenant's service jacket had been eye opening. Vandy grad with honors just before turning twenty and then immediately entering the Corps. She had excelled in basic training, and OCS. Now, almost two years later, she was considered a specialist in forensics with superior performance reviews every six months. Fluent in Spanish, passable in several forms of Arabic, and she graded sharpshooter in almost every weapon the Corps offered ratings in. The girl was on her way up in a hurry. Definitely not a typical Article 32 defendant!

So how could she have wound up in so much hot water? It made absolutely no sense at all. Amanda decided she had to start somewhere. A.J. wanted a computer. Three phone calls later, she had a laptop located and had sent a runner to pick it up. She sat at her gray steel desk and propped her feet up on it with her office door closed, a yellow legal pad in her lap.

From top to bottom on the left under a heading were the charges against Moring. The center column read "person accusing." Only two right now, the captain and the major. The last column on the right was headed "Possible defenses or mitigating circumstances." It was of course completely blank. For some reason, Amanda thought better chewing a number two pencil. She was amazed her lips weren't already yellow on this case.

Her phone rang; she was so engrossed in staring at her legal pad her mind had gone to autopilot. "Jernigan," she replied.

A woman was on the other end of the phone. "Is this Captain Amanda Jernigan?"

"Yes, who's speaking?"

"May I assume you are representing Lieutenant Moring?"

Amanda was sitting up straight now; this was the phone call A.J. was talking about. "Yes, but unless you want me to hang up, I need to know who I'm speaking to."

"Captain Jernigan, there are several people needing to speak to you. Do you have a secure line available?"

'Yes. This is the JAG office, of course we have secure lines."

"Excellent. So you'll be sure we are who we say we are, please hang up. Pull out a phone book and look up the number for the Federal Bureau of Investigation in Quantico, Virginia. When the receptionist comes on the line, ask for Assistant Director King. Goodbye, Captain."

The woman terminated the call. *There's certainly a lot more to Lt. Moring than meets the eye*. Amanda pulled out the D.C. area phone book and turned to "Federal Government" listings as fast as she could turn the pages. Five minutes later, the captain was holding for Assistant Director King.

"Captain Jernigan, Tony King here. I have you on speakerphone. Linda Kowalski and Thomas Hendrix are with me. Linda is one of our top analysts, Thomas is actually retired, and he held my position until recently. We'd like to ask you some questions about Lt. Moring."

"Mr. King, in the first place, I'd be unable to answer any questions about my client, and second, why does the FBI have an interest in this case?"

"Good answer, good question, Captain. First, the FBI has no official interest in this case whatsoever. The more we look into the case, that could change, but for now, no official interest. The three of us in this room are all close friends of Lt. Moring's parents. We consider ourselves friends of A.J. as well. A few days ago, Linda received an urgent package from Lt. Moring indicating she had reason to believe she was about to be in trouble and needed help. She also sent a floppy disc.

"Since we've become involved, we've attempted to contact the other members of her unit. We've been stymied, but Mr. Hendrix has a number of friends in the military that owe him, shall we say favors? We'll be contacting them. We also tried to contact A.J. We traced her to Cali, Colombia, but she had already been moved to Gitmo before we could contact her. Is she being detained?"

"Officially it's termed confined to quarters. Actually she's being held in solitary confinement in the basement of the BOQ in Gitmo. As far as I know, I'm the only person she can talk to."

"What has she told you?"

"Nothing, nada. She told me she can't trust anyone. She did tell me today to go back to my office and wait for a phone call. I'm assuming this is that call?"

"It definitely is Captain. We have a copy of her after-action report. It makes very interesting reading. If we can get corroboration, it's going to paint Captain Morris and Major Lewis in a very bad light."

Hendrix spoke up. "Amanda, this is Thomas Hendrix. How many Article 32s have you been involved with?"

"Uh, this is my second, Mr. Hendrix."

"Does that seem odd to you, Amanda?"

"It didn't, Mr. Hendrix, but it's looking odd now, sir."

"Amanda, please call me Thomas. I hope we're going to be seeing a lot of each other. Would you consider having me on the defense team? Second chair of course."

"Mr. Hen…Thomas, I think I could use the help, and I'm sure A.J. will be glad to have you."

"Great. Here's what we're proposing. My friends and I are running down witnesses to bolster A.J.'s version of the events. We're making good headway. When you arrive at your quarters tonight, a courier will deliver some files including a fax copy of Lt. Moring's after-action report. I believe you'll be surprised. Today, please advise the hearing officer you'll have a co-counsel. Don't use my name just yet, only that I've been requested by the defendant."

"Mr. Hendrix, they'll want more information than that."

"They may want it, but they can't require it. Tell them I'm licensed to practice in The Commonwealth of Virginia and the District of Columbia. That's all they have to know right now. I'll be heading out for Gitmo in the next twelve hours. We have a few more loose ends to run down on this end. Please, Amanda, tell A.J. you spoke to us and help is on the way. And tell her that her parents don't know."

"I don't understand. Why wouldn't she want her parents to know?"

Linda spoke up now. "Amanda, do you have any idea who A.J.'s parents are?"

"No, like I said, she won't tell me anything. She just keeps saying she needs a laptop."

"A.J. is a remarkable young woman, but it's no wonder. Her mother is arguably the most influential investigative reporter in Washington, and her dad is a consultant for the Bureau and has been involved in cases so secret it would make people think they were reading some Tom Clancy novel if they heard about them. Let me put it this way. Sometimes the president calls them just to see how they're doing, and that's when he doesn't need a favor. A.J. knew if her parents get involved, this thing might get blown way out of proportion. She's smart. If you can get her to talk, listen to her.

"I will. Thanks for calling me, all of you. And thanks for trusting me. Right or wrong, I want my client to get fair treatment. That's what matters."

"Good. File the motion, read the file, and go see A.J. Oh, and get her a damned laptop, okay?"

"I will, I'll do it all. Good to speak to you all, and Mr. Hen…Thomas, I'll be seeing you soon." The call terminated. *This is going to be a case to tell my friends about. Oh wait, I probably won't be able to tell a soul. If I did, I'd have to kill them.* She threw the legal pad in her briefcase. It would be filling up tonight. A smile began to appear on her face. This case had the potential to be interesting. Extremely interesting.

CHAPTER 8

Guantanamo Bay, Cuba

Hearing Room B

"Ten-hut! Lt. General Gaines presiding. This hearing is back in session. Please be seated." The court administrator took his seat.

A.J. took in her surroundings again. It didn't look much like a TV courtroom. Fluorescent lighting, puke green walls with what looked like pine wainscoting. Wood floors that appeared to have been polished weekly for thirty years. The air conditioning struggled with the dense, tropical air. Two black ceiling fans whirled furiously, one wandering with an off-balance blade.

She was seated at the long, plain wood defense table. Amanda was on her left, Thomas Hendrix on her right. It was good to see Thomas; he had always been like an uncle to A.J. He understood her, just as he understood her parents; and he had always accepted her family as if they were part of his own. A.J. felt closer to Linda, but it was only a matter of degree. Actually, A.J. didn't really feel "close" to anyone.

A.J. thought Amanda looked tired and had told her so before the hearing started. "I'm sorry, A.J., I am. Thomas and I have been up all night laying out your defense. He's actually a pretty damned good attorney. It's also a plus because he's always been on the prosecution side. He's been picking me apart and then helping with the right response. I'm impressed. You should be getting a damned medal, not up on charges. By the way, you choose your friends well. Hendrix has witnesses that will blow the prosecution out of the water. Sit back and watch."

So she did. The first half of the morning segment went almost exactly as Capt. Jernigan said it would. The prosecutor, another JAG captain named Preston Goode, outlined the charges. Then he called Capt. Morris. Morris basically recited a sanitized version of the mission. He had admitted taking a wrong turn, which surprised A.J. From there on out, his account was a novel. His Toyota had struck a mine, he had been in shock, A.J. had slapped him, taken over the unit. She had called off a helicopter extraction, and the unit had to be rescued by Colombian Army units.

Capt. Jernigan was asked if she wanted to cross-examine Morris. She deferred, reserving the right to recall Morris later. Morris and the prosecutor acted smugly satisfied.

Major Lewis had been called next. His testimony was relatively brief. Lt. Moring had been instructed to file an after-action report by 0500 hours, and she failed to do so. When he had verbally reprimanded her, she exploded in curses and in a distinctly insubordinate manner. When he completed his testimony, the general turned to Cap. Jernigan and asked if she had any questions.

"Actually, I do, sir. Just a few." Jernigan stood, walked halfway to the witness chair, and began in a voice that sounded slightly tentative. "Major Lewis, do you think there's any chance you could have been mistaken about Lt. Moring not submitting an after-action report?"

"Captain Jernigan, are you seriously asking me that? I mean, do you think I just forgot?" He glared at Jernigan, his facial muscles straining.

"No, Major, I suppose you didn't just forget you got the report or lost it or anything like that. Now, Major, one more time for the record, what time did these events take place?"

"Approximately 0515 hours."

In that timid, nervous voice, Jernigan posed another question. "So, Major, there's no possibility you could be mistaken about the time either?"

Major Lewis flew to his feet. "Young lady, I'm tired of your accusations. Marine Corps majors don't make stupid mistakes like that!"

"Major!" General Gaines barked, "This is a room full of officers. I expect, no, I insist on professionalism here. Be seated and calm down, or *you* will have made a stupid mistake! Please continue, Captain Jernigan."

"Ahem… so, Major, you are telling this court that the alleged infraction and insubordination occurred at approximately 0515 hours?"

"That is correct."

"Then Lt. Moring was placed under arrest and confined to quarters at approximately 0515 hours?"

"Lt. Moring was actually never arrested. I told her that she was confined to quarters pending this hearing. She was escorted to her quarters and detained there."

"Would it also be correct to state, Major, that between the time the lieutenant left your office, under guard, and the time she arrived at her quarters, her room had already been searched, and a laptop, printer, and camera, all personal property of Lt. Moring, had been removed and have still not been returned to her?"

"I couldn't say."

Amanda turned to the General. "General, for the record, Lt. Moring has been confined to her quarters either in Cali or here at Gitmo until this hearing."

The general nodded to Jernigan. The prosecutor rose. "Your honor, the prosecution stipulates the defendant has been confined since 0515 hours on the morning these events took place. Might we ask where counsel is going with this?"

Amanda turned to the prosecution table. She seemed to have grown taller and in a clear, authoritative tone replied, "Where counsel is going with this is that our contention is that an after-action report *was* submitted, it was submitted *on time*, and that, unlike the piece of fiction recited by Capt. Morris, it was a *true and accurate* accounting of the events of the previous eighteen hours. And we will be submitting evidence and testimony to prove our contention!"

The room was silent. Everyone not seated at the defense table looked stunned. "Your honor, I believe the defense counsel has just claimed two Marine officers are liars," Goode stated quietly.

"Sir, the defense intends to supply evidence and testimony to what actually took place. We intend to leave it up to you who is telling the truth and who is lying."

The general looked at Captain Jernigan and asked, "Is the defense finished with their cross of Major Lewis?"

"Oh no, Your Honor, we aren't through by any means. May we assume the prosecution is finished with their presentation of charges and evidence?"

The prosecutor stood and nodded in the affirmative.

"At this time, I would like my co-counsel, Mr. Thomas Hendrix, to present our opening evidence, namely the content of the after-action report submitted by Lt. Moring. We would like to address the charges related to the after-action report first. The content of Lt. Moring's report has a large and direct bearing on the other charges before this court."

Hendrix winked at A.J. and stood with his hands full of documents. He proceeded to the prosecutor's table and deposited one pile then walked to the table before the general. He laid several sheets of paper before the general.

"Sir, this is a copy of Lt. Moring's after-action report. We'd like to submit it as defense exhibit one. I say it's a *copy* because we have no way to know what happened to the original."

"General, I must object. This report could have been printed this morning for all we know." The prosecutor was standing, waving the report in the air.

"General, Captain Goode is most astute. These copies *were* printed this morning. It's what they were printed *from* that makes them credible." He laid a floppy disc on the General's table. "We'd like this computer disc labeled as defense exhibit two. It was received via U.S. mail in Alexandria, Virginia; approximately thirty-six hours after the incidents outlined in the defendant's report took place. Since Major Lewis has told us the defendant has been in custody since the meeting in his office, it is obvious this disc was encoded prior to her being placed under arrest. The disc contains not only the lieutenant's after-action report, but also her previous after-action reports for a month previous to the report in question. We have also included a chain of custody form for the disc as well as a report from Electronic Data Systems. Their report indicates the disc was encoded on a computer of the type owned by the defendant, and that the data on the disc was written to this disc at 0430 hours. Well in advance of the 0515 time the major here has twice verified."

The room was silent. The general and the prosecutor were reviewing the report. Captain Goode rose. "General, I object!"

The general glanced up briefly from the report. "To what, Captain Goode?"

"Well, I wasn't provided a copy of this report to review."

"General, first, the disc was only received last night when Mr. Hendrix arrived from D.C. Second, there's no obligation for discovery on either side for an Article 32. I would note the prosecution didn't provide what Capt. Miller or Major Lewis's testimony would be."

"Your objection is overruled, Captain Goode. This court is in recess; I want to review this evidence. We'll reconvene about 1330 hours. Dismissed."

A.J., Jernigan, and Hendrix went to Jernigan's office to eat. Hendrix and Amanda didn't want to run into the prosecution, Miller, or the major. Amanda had run by the break room and bought some really crappy sandwiches.

"Amanda, how are we doing?" A.J. asked.

"She's doing great, A.J." Hendrix answered. "She's done exactly what we talked about last night. We agreed someone picked Amanda because she was green. They expected her to do a rookie job. Then she lulled them to sleep and got Lewis to show his ass before she lowered the boom on them. As long as the general isn't in on the fix, I think we're in great shape. I don't think he'll have a problem finding a court martial isn't appropriate. His problem will be cleaning up the mess Miller and Lewis created."

"Thank you, Thomas, you too, Amanda. I'm just tired of it. I'd almost plead out just to make it all go away, but it would break my dad's heart."

"A.J., that's the first time you've mentioned your family. Are you sure we can't let them know something?"

"Sure, once it's over. So, Thomas, did you and Linda call in the big guns in one of those top secret meeting rooms at Quantico?"

Amanda looked between Hendrix and A.J. with question marks written all over her forehead.

Hendrix looked at Amanda. "You'd have no way of knowing, Amanda, but she's right. You see, A.J.'s parents have been in some very secret shit at our Quantico installation. Stuff you'd never believe even if I could tell you. And that was before A.J. here was born. We're almost like family."

Amanda nodded. "Then she called the right people for help. Thomas, how did you ever get our witnesses here, and where are they? When I tried to find them, they had all turned into ghosts."

"I didn't tell you this, but seeing as how we're actually in a base on Cuban territory, there just happens to be a CIA installation here on the base. They're camped out there until we re-convene. I didn't want anybody on the other side to know we were able to find the witnesses and get them here. As far as how we found them, probably the less you know, the better."

Amanda looked between A.J. and Hendrix. "You people are quite something. I've looked over A.J.'s jacket. What I see is a truly remarkable woman, a credit to the Corps. For reasons yet to be determined, someone tried to screw her. She sends one letter and half the FBI is on the case. Remarkable, really, it is. For some reason, I feel like I should have an automatic dislike for the both of you. It doesn't show in your jacket, but I'm led to believe you, A.J., are from very serious money. And you, Mr. Hendrix, you're a pretty good lawyer, who just happens to have been an assistant FBI director. I'm dealing with some very exclusive people. Instead, I feel the opposite. You're both totally normal, likeable people. I hope we pull this off."

"Amanda, by now you should have figured out I'm far from normal. I realize I have issues, issues with trust, people, shit like that. But I understand it, and I try to compensate. My parents are the ones you need to meet. You'd never guess in a million years what they've done. For this country."

"She's right." Hendrix nodded. "Her parents live on a farm forty-five minutes from D.C., and they're nothing like the Washington establishment. People in D.C. seem to like to run around and stab people in the back. Steve and Samantha both will just walk up and stab you in the chest. You'd like them, I really believe it."

Two knocks hit Amanda's door. "Capt. Jernigan, the general wants to start up again."

Jernigan turned to the others. "Well, lets go then!" and led them out her door and down the long linoleum corridor. As she walked, she had noticed a thirtyish young man in a black suit and tie standing in the hall. Hendrix had nodded at the young man, who spun and took off. She looked at Hendrix quizzically, and he just returned an enigmatic smile and gave her a thumbs-up sign.

After the hearing was re-convened, General Gaines directed his attention to Amanda. “Captain Jernigan, I’ve reviewed Lt. Moring’s report and the supporting documentation. I can’t say I’ve ever seen a case with such a huge disparity between the two sides of the story. You stated earlier you could support the lieutenant’s position with evidence and testimony. I assume we’ve seen the evidence. Will the lieutenant be testifying?”

“Certainly, General, however, unless there are objections, we would prefer to open with testimony from the defense witnesses.”

At that point Captain Goode shot to his feet, his chair propelled backward at high velocity. “General, I have to object. There were no witnesses on the defense pre-hearing documents!” Captain Miller and Major Lewis were having an animated, private conversation as well.

“General, our witnesses were very difficult to locate. They only arrived today. However, there’s no prohibition I’m aware of to calling witnesses to support the evidence submitted, namely the lieutenant’s after-action report.”

“Agreed, Capt. Jernigan. I’d like you to tell me who these witnesses are and where they are at this moment.”

Hendrix stood. “General, as to their location, our witnesses are being brought to the hallway outside this hearing room as we speak. Their identities are as follows: we have a Sargent Vasquez, Corporal Moreno…”

“General, we would object to these witnesses!”

“On what grounds, Captain?”

Goode was shifting back and forth. He sounded tentative. “Uh, General, we would contend that these two enlisted men are known to have a rather low opinion of Capt. Miller. Further, they are considered to be friendly toward Lt. Moring.”

Amanda spoke up. “So the prosecution is contending these two witnesses would perjure themselves?”

Hendrix turned to the general. “Sir, while you’re considering that point, I’d like to finish my witness list. We don’t concede the two witnesses we mentioned could have bias, but we have more. Also waiting in the hall are the aircraft commanders of the Spectre gunship and the Pave Low helicopter mentioned in Lt. Moring’s report. The Lt. has never met these men. We also have the crew chief from the Pave low. He had one short conversation with the lieutenant. Last, we have one of the DEA agents on this mission. For security reasons, I can only identify him as “Tom”. This agent also has several copies of his own after-action report. That report is classified, and I would point out the defense has not even seen this report.”

The general leaned back in his chair; he waved his hand across his graying crew cut and shook his head. Then he stood and walked to the window without saying a word. Finally he turned to the room. “Clear the hearing room, and bring in this “Tom” guy. Captain Goode, don’t even think about objecting.”

Everyone filed out quietly. Once they were in the hall, the two opposing sides took up positions about twenty feet apart; the witnesses were all missing. They must have been removed to yet another location. Just as A.J. turned to ask Amanda a question, she saw Tom coming down the hall. He was wearing a suit and carrying a briefcase. As he walked by A.J.'s group, he winked at her. "It's gonna be fine, A.J., don't sweat it."

He walked into the hearing room, and a guard closed the door and stood in the hall outside.

"Well, Amanda, is he right?"

"I think so. All we've ever discussed is if we can get the truth out, the worst thing you did was slap Miller, and he was non-responsive at the time, so it was justified."

Hendrix smiled at her. "It'll be okay. Let's go sit down." The three walked a few feet down the hall to a wooden bench and took a seat. There was surprisingly little conversation. Everyone was tense and tired.

Ten long minutes later, there was a knock on the hearing room door. The guard opened it and walked down to the three. "The general wants to see you three inside please." Captain Goode and his group had walked down the hall toward them and heard the guard's instruction. The guard turned to Goode and said, "Sorry, Captain, he was specific, defense team only."

A.J. and her group filed into the hearing room. The general and Tom were seated at the defense table engaged in conversation. The general motioned A.J. to be seated but held his hand up to Hendrix and Amanda. "I'd really like to speak to the lieutenant in private."

"Uh, General, with all due respect, as the lieutenant's counsel, I'm forced to advise her against doing that, sir." Amanda sounded a little nervous, but still held her ground.

"I understand, Captain. I'd have thought less of you if you hadn't made that statement. My preference is to speak to you alone, Lieutenant, but Captain Jernigan is right. You have the right to have your counsel here, both of them if you like."

A.J. looked at the general. She looked in his eyes, and Tom's. She saw nothing negative. She had inherited the ability from her father; it was a nearly uncanny knack for seeing deception from facial features. She didn't understand how it worked, nor did her father. They both just knew that it did. She turned to Amanda and Hendrix. "It's okay. We've got this. Will you two please wait for me?"

Hendrix and the captain nodded and left the room. General Gaines waited for the door to close and turned to A.J. "Lieutenant, you have planted a huge problem in my lap. What? Do you find that amusing, Lieutenant?" A.J. realized there must have been a hint of a smile on her face.

"Oh no, sir, sorry. Ironic maybe, but no, I didn't think you were amusing."

"Ironic?"

"Yes, sir, those were almost the exact words Major Lewis used when he read my report."

"Humph, well, young lady, while I can certainly sympathize with how he must have felt, I can't say much for how he chose to fix his problem. What really happened in his office, Alexandra?"

At that moment, Tom elbowed the general and shook his head rather violently.

"What? What did I say?"

"General, I'm told the lieutenant prefers not to be called Alexandra. I was told it usually results in a swift blow to the back of the head. Presumably that only applied to enlisted grades and DEA agents."

"Don't worry, General, you're safe," A.J. stated. All three laughed.

"Good to know, Lieutenant. You're sitting here for slapping one superior officer already! Now, back to what happened in Major Lewis's office."

"He wanted me to change my report, sir. He told me if I'd write one up along the lines of what Captain Morris did, he could let me off with a warning. I told him I wouldn't fabricate a report, and it pretty much went downhill from there."

"I suspected something along those lines. Did you really refer to Morris as Captain Crunch?"

"I'm afraid so, sir. It was wrong. I shouldn't have done that. He just drove me so crazy, sir…"

"I understand, Lieutenant. Morris is an idiot. From what I've heard, and from Tom's report here, the Corps made a huge error when we let Morris do anything but push paper. Lewis is another matter. I'm afraid I'm going to have to deal with him. Whatever else happens, we'll need to make some major changes in Cali. I'm tempted to pull everybody out and start over. We're not supposed to have any military personnel in there anyway. You are my immediate problem. I thought I had two choices, promote you with a commendation letter, or give you a quick and dirty discharge of some kind. Anything in between just didn't work. I couldn't just send you back to your unit like nothing ever happened. Then Tom here made a suggestion. The more I think about it, the more I like it. Tell her, Tom."

"Basically I want you to come to work for me. You'd be doing black work. Undercover stuff. I've seen you in action. You're smart, resourceful; you've got bigger cajones than most men I know. You're fluent in Spanish, and you're deadly when it's needed."

"But what about the Corps?"

General Gaines smiled, “ I hate to lose you, but I think this is a good deal for both of us. You’ll still be working for the government; in fact, Tom’s giving you a big bump as far as pay is concerned. Your jacket is going to say you were given an administrative discharge. There’ll be a glowing letter in it if someone has a top-secret clearance. Basically you’ll disappear to the military. It’s a good deal for both you and Tom, and it’ll make my life simpler. Do you need to think about it?”

A.J. stood; she walked to the same window the general had stared out of. ”So, Tom, you don’t really work for the DEA, do you?”

“No, how did you know?”

“I’m not sure. You work for someone else. The DEA is a cover. It’s like you’re hiding in plain sight. Just tell me one thing. If I say yes, are we the good guys?”

“Yes, you have my word.”

“Okay then, we have a deal.” She walked back to the table and shook Tom’s hand. She stood at attention and saluted the general. He jumped up and snapped off a sharp salute.

“Are we done then? Can I go?”

Tom stood. “Yes. I guess we’ll be in touch to arrange transportation. Will you be at the BOQ?”

“Yes, she will,” The general replied, “and not in the basement. I’ll arrange everything. I’m very glad to have met you, Lt. Moring.”

A.J. nodded and turned. She walked out the door and looked for Amanda and Hendrix. As she walked toward them, she could see concern on their faces.

“How did it go?” Amanda asked.

"It's fine, it's all over. There was never a hearing, and I'm no longer a Marine. I'll be working for Tom." She looked to Amanda. "Could I get a ride to the BOQ?"

Amanda nodded. "Sure, I'd be glad to. Is there anything else we could help you with?"

"Great, one more thing, could I use your office phone?"

"Sure, let's go."

When they got to Amanda's office, A.J. turned to Hendrix and Jernigan. "Thank you both. I assume I dial nine; is there a prefix for the States?"

Amanda filled her in.

A.J. went into Amanda's office, closed the door, and sat at Amanda's gray metal desk. She picked up the phone and dialed a series of numbers. A woman answered after three rings. "Hello?"

"Hi, Mom, it's me."

CHAPTER 9

Puerto Vallarta, Mexico

A.J. walked from the plane toward the terminal. It was hot. Her jeans and a spiffy tee shirt had not been an ideal choice, but she was short on clothing. As she lined up for customs in the terminal, she felt mild anxiety.

Any time she traveled as a Marine, she had been carrying a red passport because of being a DOD employee. The red passport was a mixed blessing. When returning to the States, it was great. She would be waved through lines; her luggage was never checked. The downside was her fellow DOD employees called the red passport a "bullet in the head passport." Several recent overseas hijackings had resulted in red passport holders being the first passengers to be shot. Or beaten and then shot. Hijackers seemed to collect passports early to evaluate who was onboard.

This time, her passport was green. It also called out her new identity, Anna Juanita Dejesus. It showed a home address of Miami, Florida. A.J. *had* flown in from Miami after leaving Gitmo. Her visit to Gitmo had been, well, memorable. After the hearing, she had returned to the BOQ. Her new room had been a big improvement. It was no longer in the basement, and it had a pretty decent view.

A few hours after the close of the hearing, she had visitors. Amanda and Mr. Hendrix had stopped by. Amanda had A.J.'s laptop and camera, and Hendrix had her duffel bag and a cooler of beer.

"Have you called your parents?" Hendrix asked a couple beers into the visit.

"I called my mother. I told her I had been in a firefight, and then I kinda glossed over the hearing. I told her I was being transferred, but I didn't know what my final destination would be yet. I promised I'd let her know. I did tell her I'd been in a bit of a jam, and you and Linda had come to my rescue. I failed to mentioned I'd been thrown out of the Corps."

"I'm headed back to D.C. tonight. Would you mind if I fill Steve and Sam in?"

"I guess not, Mr. Hendrix. They'll find out eventually I'm sure. Maybe you can make it sound more palatable. Think you can keep them from using the nuclear option?"

Hendrix laughed. "I think so. I'll tell T.D. first. He'll probably be able to give me some advice."

"T.D.'s your older brother, right?" Amanda asked.

"Yeah, he's weird like me. He's scary smart, and a nerd, but he gets along with people a lot better than me."

Amanda laughed. "You get along with some people. You grew on me." She went to the cooler and grabbed another beer. She looked at the other two and, after some nods, wound up bringing back three. "What does your brother do?"

"Computers," A.J. replied after a swallow. "He graduated from MIT. He fooled around with that Microsoft guy, but then he went to work for No Such Agency. Now he can't tell me a damned thing about what he does, but he could probably tell you what color underwear we're all wearing."

Hendrix and Amanda both laughed. "Well, don't be surprised if you don't get to talk to him a lot more soon. The way Tom was talking, your clearance is going to be a lot higher very soon. By the way, that's part of why we're here." He reached in his briefcase and pulled out a large manila folder. "Tom had to leave, but he said to give you this. Please don't open it until we leave; it's classified. I don't want to know about the contents. He said he'd be seeing you in about a week. There are supposed to be airline tickets in here, and he said he'd meet up with you there. Wherever "there" is."

The man in the immigration line looked at A.J.'s passport and asked her in decent English, "Are you here for business or pleasure, Miss Dejesus? A.J. replied "pleasure" in perfect Spanish. The man nodded, stamped her passport, and welcomed her to Mexico in Spanish as well. Tom's note in the envelope had instructed her to not speak English anywhere in public; this stop in Puerto Vallarta would be a mini vacation as well as the beginning of establishing her cover for her new job.

A.J. walked with her carry-on through the airport admiring the beautiful marble floors. Stonework was plentiful and cheap in Central America, but that didn't detract from its beauty. She by-passed baggage claim since there was nothing to claim and proceeded to the queue of taxis. Once assigned a cab by the "taxi boss", she asked him to carry her to the Fiesta Americana Hotel. He nodded and left the airport at near warp speed.

The scenery on the road was unlike Colombia. The coastal area here on the Pacific was flat, with low, jungle-covered mountains just a mile or so inshore. The air was warm, and humid, but even in the un-air-conditioned cab, it wasn't unpleasantly hot. The airport was several kilometers north of "town," and she began to notice a gradual increase in buildings and people.

The entire atmosphere was rather new. Similar to Colombia, yet altogether different. Colombia seemed to be a country with a sharp division of classes. There were the extremely wealthy, living in palatial apartments or on secluded estates, and then the poor. The rich were attended to as well as guarded by serfs. The rest of the population seemed to be living in a time warp, clothed, working, and existing much as they had one hundred years ago. There seemed to be no middle class.

She looked at her cab driver. He was well dressed, didn't smell, and seemed happy. A crucifix hung from his mirror, a statue of the Virgin Mary was firmly attached to his dash, and Mexican pop music blared from a recent-looking Pioneer radio.

Soon the cab turned off the main road down a long, palm-lined driveway. Apparently they were arriving at her destination. She noted the landscaping was immaculate. At the end of the drive, the cab pulled up to a 180-degree curve at the entrance. The lobby seemed to be a good three meters higher than the road with ceramic tile and marble steps. She turned to pay the driver, asking how much.

"Three dollars U.S., senorita," he replied. She handed him a five, expecting him to keep the change. He quickly pulled two ones out and explained it was not "customary" to tip a driver unless he performed some extra service. A.J. thought that seemed at odds with how everything else worked in Central America. Having paid her cab fare, she had reached for her single bag when a young man in a hotel uniform grabbed it.

"Checking in, senorita?" he asked.

"Sí," she replied, remembering to stay in character. He escorted her through the lobby to the check-in counter. The lobby was remarkable! It was a palapa hut, but it was thirty meters tall and about the same diameter. There were no doors; she could plainly see the Pacific Ocean out the backside of the palapa. There was no air conditioning, but the shade, the breeze, and the smooth, marble floors all seemed to contribute to a very comfortable setting. Her jeans and tee shirt felt perfect.

When greeted by the young girl behind the counter, A.J. indicated she had a reservation in the name of Dejesus. Since she had addressed the desk clerk in Spanish, she replied accordingly, "Miss Dejesus, your room is not quite ready. We can take your bag and deliver it to your room, or you can keep it with you as you prefer. Please go to the bar and enjoy a beverage on the house while you are waiting. It should be only a matter of a few minutes." She handed A.J. two drink tokens and pointed her toward the bar.

A.J. wasn't a big drinker; she had found she enjoyed alcohol, perhaps too much. Samantha had been frank and honest with her daughter about her struggle with drinking. She told her daughter she could control it now, but there had been a time when it definitely controlled her. Nearly to the point of destroying her. A.J. had appreciated her mother's honesty, and since it was widely reported the problem could be hereditary, she had always been cautious about her drinking. It didn't seem like today would be a problem. She walked to the large bar and took a seat on a wicker, upholstered stool. She had a simply gorgeous view of the ocean, a seat in the shady palapa, and a piña colada. After the last week, she allowed her mind to zone out.

"Do you mind if I sit here?"

The question startled A.J. She turned to her left to see a woman, a very beautiful woman. The woman was obviously South or Central American, A.J. suspected Venezuelan but was uncertain. What was slightly surprising was the question to A.J. had been in flawless English.

"Sure, no problem," A.J. replied in Spanish.

"May I join you? You look like you've had a long journey," the girl stated. *Well, it begins.* A.J. instantly recognized the beginning of the verbal dance of passwords Tom had given her. It had seemed rather TVish to A.J. Seriously, wasn't there a more efficient way to insure the two "spies" were who they were supposed to be?

"Yes, it was a long journey." Once again, the question in English, the reply in Spanish.

"How was your flight, Anna? I'm Isobel." This time, she was speaking Spanish. She extended her hand to A.J., and they shook.

"It was fine."

"Why don't we go to your room, so we can speak more privately?" Isobel asked.

"It isn't ready," A.J. replied.

"Of course it is." Isobel laughed. "It's been ready. That was just an arrangement I made with the desk clerk to give me an opportunity to make sure you were the right girl, and that you hadn't been followed."

"So we're good then?"

"Yes, let's go. You can bring your drink if you'd like."

Isobel threw a few dollars on the bar and pointed A.J. toward the elevators. They rode to the top floor, exited, and turned left. All the room doors were on the left. The corridor was open air with the entry road and its landscaping on the right. The omnipresent marble was on the floor here too. The pair walked all the way to the end of the hall. Here, however, the double doors met them head-on. Isobel inserted a key and opened the door, beckoning A.J. in.

"Well, welcome to your home for a week or so, Anna. What do you think?" Isobel did a twirl, showing off a huge living area to what was obviously a suite. There were private balconies overlooking the Pacific, each with a planter of yellow hibiscus.

A.J. took it all in, the room, the view, the 151 coursing through her veins.

"Holy shit! You mean I'll have to leave in a week?"

CHAPTER 10

Puerto Vallarta, Mexico

“So, Anna, let’s go on a tour!” Isobel walked her through the two-bedroom suite. She showed A.J. her bedroom, the largest and nicest one. It had its own patio and a spa tub out on the patio. Isobel showed A.J. another bedroom, which Isobel had already moved into. They wound up back in the huge main room. It had three conversation areas, each with couches and chairs or loveseats. There was a dining area with a glass table and seating for six. “The hotel has two suites like this one, This is the nicer of the two in my opinion. We face toward the city, and when the sun goes down, we can see the lights of the city. It’s very beautiful.” Isobel sat down. A.J. started to sit. “No. Stand, please. This is one of my jobs, I have to pick out some clothing and a new look for you.”

"What's wrong with my look?" A.J. looked toward a mirrored wall. Okay, she saw a twenty-three-year-old girl with very short brown hair. No makeup, a white tee shirt with a scoop neck, and jeans that were neither tight nor baggy. She looked at her leather, practical sandals. She failed to see a problem.

"Anna, do me a favor. Walk to the bar over there, turn, and come back please." Isobel watched carefully as A.J. did as she was asked. "You know, you can tell a great deal about an individual's personality just by their walk."

"I'm sure. So what does my walk reveal, pray tell?"

"It tells me you are confident, self-assured. You are athletic, and you walk just like a man."

"Isobel, for Christ's sake, I'm a freakin Marine, or was. I grew up on a farm! What did you and Tom expect?"

"Mr. Tom is an excellent judge of character. He sees the type of character he is looking for in you. He knows you can shoot; he knows you can think and act under pressure. But Mr. Tom sees all of us as assets, with many different uses. That's my job. By the time our employer gets here, I am supposed to have you prepared for anything from showing off your charms by the pool to looking stunning in an evening gown. Can you guess where we'll have to start?"

"No, but I'm pretty sure I'm not going to like it!"

"Have a seat, I'll be right back." Isobel disappeared into her room. A.J. could hear her rummaging around for a few moments. She returned, took a seat next to A.J., and placed a box on her lap. "Okay, kick off your shoes and try these on."

"Heels? Really? I hate heels; I've worn them like three times in my life. Did you know they're designed by men to torture women?"

"You are so wrong. Did you know almost every woman in this part of the world wears heels? Every day? Does your mother wear heels?"

"Yes, but…"

"Do you think your dad wants to torture your mom?"

Better not answer that one! "No, but…"

"But nothing. Women wear heels because it makes their legs and their asses look better, plain and simple."

"What's wrong with my ass?'

"I have no idea, probably nothing, but who could tell in those farmer pants you're wearing!" Isobel handed A.J. a bag. "Go to your room. Put on this swimsuit and cover-up. And the heels. We're going to the pool. Your room key is on your dresser; it's on a long chain. Wear it around your neck so you can order drinks and charge them to our room. Now hurry! I'm thirsty, and we have more lessons for you today!"

A.J. glared at Isobel for a full thirty seconds then turned and stomped into her room. She fumed internally as she undressed. The bikini was small, but not obscene. The cover-up matched the yellow bikini and was designed like a short gown. The shoes were metallic silver and were strappy sandals with three-inch heels. That was about the same height she usually had seen her mother in. *Why could Tom possibly care about this shit?* She fumed, but remembered what Tom had said in his note; she should consider Isobel as a trainer for skills that could be needed.

"All right, let's go to the pool."

Isobel watched A.J. walk to the door. "No, no, no, A.J., that will never do. Follow me to the elevator, try to copy me. One foot before the other, a slight hip toss with each step. You're still trying to walk like you're in combat boots."

A.J. did her best to copy Isobel, and soon they were lying by the pool, sipping more drinks.

"When we get back to the room and you've showered, we're going to work on some makeup. Do you ever wear any?"

"Hell no, I need my unit to respect me. I don't need them wanting to screw me. What's with all this? Does Tom expect me to be a hooker for the government?"

Isobel sat up and turned to A.J. with a serious look on her face. She broke into English in a low voice. "Anna, let's straighten this out now. Tom does not need to hire prostitutes. When we need hookers, we rent them. You may not realize it, but an expensive prostitute is considered a semi-respectable profession in this culture, as are mistresses. You'll be working undercover. Sometimes that means you'll be in a jungle somewhere with mosquitos trying to suck every last drop of blood out of your body. Sometimes you may be impersonating a hotel maid. But sometimes you'll be meeting very important people in exclusive nightclubs or mansions. As to what you'll be doing in all those places, that is Mr. Tom's place to tell you."

"But what about sex? Am I going to be expected to screw these guys for information?"

"Let me answer your question with my own personal history in that regard. I have *never* had sex with any man I didn't *choose* to screw; and in most cases, I screwed them in more than one way! So, I suppose you'll need to answer that question yourself." She rolled over in the lounger and lay on her stomach to catch the last rays as the clouds lined up over the bay. "Shut up and drink. It's three o'clock, and the rains will be getting here any time."

CHAPTER 11

Puerto Vallarta, Mexico

The rest of the week flew by. Isobel had taken A.J. for a haircut, dresses, sportswear, more swimsuits, and, of course, lingerie.

"Isobel, you realize this stuff is uncomfortable as shit, don't you? I mean, how can having a skinny piece of lace buried in your ass be considered comfortable? I'd rather just go without."

"That's always an option. You can really get a guy stuttering and forgetting everything he knows if you tell him that halfway through dinner."

"I thought I'm supposed to be getting information. Him forgetting would be kinda counterproductive, don't cha think?"

Isobel laughed. "You're catching on. You're doing much better in heels by the way. Besides, we still got you a few pairs of your traditional undies and a couple sports bras as well. Next we need to look for wigs."

"Wigs? They'll be hotter than hell. What's wrong with my hair now? You've already got me dressing and made up like a tramp. I'm surprised I haven't had anyone ask me 'How much?' yet."

"All in good time. It's time to get a cab back to the hotel. You have a test tonight."

"Test? What kind of test?"

"After the rain and a nap, we're getting all gussied up. I want you to wear the black cocktail dress. We have reservations at the high-class restaurant at the hotel, and then we're going trolling for some action. And tonight, we're acting like American tourists, so English only once we get to the restaurant."

A.J. had forgotten she'd been speaking Spanish for nearly a week. Total immersion was a good teacher. Aside from one HBO channel and CNN, the TV in the room was Spanish only.

That night, as A.J. was finishing her makeup, she could hear Isobel on her cellphone. It seemed late to A.J. It was nearly nine, but the entire region thought that was dinnertime. After siesta, most people didn't get off work until about seven.

She met Isobel in the main room. Isobel told her Tom would be in after lunch tomorrow. "Okay, I guess I'm ready for dinner. I'm not too sure what you were referring to when you said we were going trolling. Could I get a little better idea how you define trolling?"

"Sure. I have a question for you first. When was the last time you were on a date?"

"Hmm…define date."

"Okay, when was the last time you got dressed up, went to dinner, dancing, conversed? I'm not even going to ask when you last got laid."

"Not sure, maybe at Vanderbilt?"

"That's what I thought. I just need to see how you handle yourself around a regular guy. You know, one that doesn't have a uniform or a weapon. Getting laid isn't required, unless you feel like it. Remember, we're Americans tonight. We've been in town to wrap up a contract for clothing sales in Miami. It's hush hush, so we can't discuss details. Work for you?"

"Sure."

Dinner was actually very good. The posh restaurant was the only air-conditioned space in the hotel other than the guest rooms. The service was impeccable. A.J. was pretty sure she hadn't used the huge array of utensils properly, but maybe no one noticed. She picked a lobster dinner, and the two girls had finished off a bottle of wine.

A.J. found it odd no one brought a check until Isobel had beckoned for it.

"I know, it's strange, but it's considered extremely rude to bring a guest a check until they request one. Dinner, especially in a place like this, is to be savored; it's an event. You'll have to get used to that," Isobel explained. "Ready to move to the bar and shake your booty?"

A.J. blushed, but she nodded.

The two moved to the lobby area closest to the pool and the bar. A band was already playing. A waiter showed them to a table and took their drink orders, a piña colada for A.J., and a coco loco for Isobel.

"Have you tried one of these, Anna?" she asked in English. "It's nothing but liquor, seven kinds. They say two or three of these and you can speak perfect Spanish."

"Yeah, I had two at the swim-up bar the other day. I couldn't speak perfect Spanish, but I think I could communicate well with a Mexican drunk!" They were both careful to talk and laugh a little too loud and got up and danced with each other once. Sure enough, within about twenty minutes, two attractive, young Latin lounge lizards had taken the bait.

About an hour and quite a few drinks and several dances later, A.J. noticed her personal lounge lizard, Enrique, was easing his hand up her leg under the table. She tactfully took his hand and placed it on the table. The two guys had carried on decent, if predictable, conversations in English, but after that, Enrique had turned to his sidekick and whispered in Spanish loud enough for A.J. to hear, "I think this one may be a dyke. Should we still take them to our room?" His partner nodded.

"Time for a bathroom run for us girls," A.J. said, standing as she spoke and nodding at Isobel. The two plotted an exit strategy in the restroom after A.J. told Isobel what Enrique had said. "Let's have some fun with them," A.J. said. Isobel stared as A.J. reached under her dress and pulled off her panties. "These things drive me crazy anyway. I'm going to hand them to Enrique when we get back to the table then ask him to dance. I'm gonna lower the boom, so be ready to make a quick exit. Unless you like your date?"

"Nah, he doesn't do anything for me. We can blow them off. I can't wait to see this. Think you can talk loud enough for me to hear too?"

A.J. nodded and stuffed her panties in her clutch purse, touched up her lipstick, and headed back to the lounge. She sat next to Enrique and leaned over to his ear. "I have a present for you!" He looked at her with a question mark on his forehead. She grabbed his right hand with her left and twisted it palm up. She deposited the wadded-up panties in his palm and whispered, “Shall we dance?”

Enrique nearly fell all over himself getting up, and he and A.J. headed out to the floor. She tolerated his grating against her front and his hands cupping her ass; after all, she *had* given him her panties. She waited until Isobel and her date were close enough to hear. She leaned toward Enrique’s ear and said, “Enrique, I have a secret!”

“What is that, Anna?”

In perfect Spanish, she said, “My secret is I’m quite fluent in Spanish, Enrique, and I heard you tell your little friend there you thought I was a dyke. Do you know what we call a guy that buys drinks for a girl for hours and can’t tell if she’s a dyke or not?”

“No,” he replied. He had switched to Spanish as well now, and his voice was increasing in volume with his anger.

“A pussy!”

“You bitch, you have insulted my manhood!” Enrique was yelling now. Everyone on the floor was listening.

“No, Enrique, you’ve been grinding your manhood at me all night. There’s really not much there to insult. Goodnight, Enrique.” She spun out of his arms and headed for the elevators with Isobel close behind. As she approached the elevator A.J. could still hear him cursing women in general, and Anna in particular.

A.J. and Isobel waited for the elevator doors to close before they burst into laughter. A.J. immediately kicked her heels off.

“Are you sure you’re not a dyke? You certainly have cajones!” A.J. laughed so hard she was about to pee.

“I’m pretty sure I’m not. Did I pass or fail my test?”

"Both, Anna, both. You'll get a pretty good report, but you may want to work on your people skills."

"That's funny. I have it on good authority I have zero people skills. I've got nowhere to go but up, right?"

Isobel nodded, still giggling. They entered their room, and Isobel headed for her bedroom. "Sleep well, remember, we meet Mr. Tom tomorrow, mucho big business, sí?"

"Sí," A.J. answered, "tomorrow."

Chapter 12

Bay of Banderas

Puerto Vallarta, Mexico

Anna/A.J. sat in a lounger on the deck of a medium-sized sports fishing boat in the bay. “Tom” was seated next to her, smoking a large Cuban cigar. Isobel was up on the bridge, entertaining the crew. A.J gazed out over the Pacific. The bay looked calm. It had a bluish-green tint other than four or five veins of red that bled clay into the bay from creeks flowing down out of the low mountains and jungles that surrounded the bay and the town as well.

Tom, Isobel, and A.J. were supposedly American tourists trolling for dorado today. Isobel was acting as if her primary objective was to get very drunk on the free alcohol furnished by the small, two-man crew, but she doubted they noticed the large amount of liquor that was “spilled” over the side.

Tom wore a garish Hawaiian shirt and shorts. Isobel and A.J. were in jean shorts with bikini tops. Isobel had told A.J. she had researched women's attire at the marina several times, and their attire was quite customary for gringo fishermen.

"A.J., I suppose you're wondering why we're out fishing today," Tom began in English. He spoke in a low voice.

"A little, but it seems like a spot that would be hard for someone to listen in?"

"Exactly! That and I love fishing. Anyway, you have to have questions. At your hearing, you asked me two questions: you wanted to know who I really worked for and were we the good guys."

A.J. nodded.

"Okay, technically I *do* work for the DEA, but you were right, it is a cover. A couple years ago, some of us in the DEA and the CIA were drinking one night, and we came to a couple conclusions. First, we agreed the 'war on drugs' had already been lost. It was a waste of money and resources. Second, we agreed the greater threat was not the drugs going into the States. The larger threat was the money leaving the States. If the money had only been making the cartels rich, that was one thing. We concluded the money was being used to make changes in the governments of the entire South and Central American region. Mexico, Colombia, Panama, Ecuador, Venezuela. The cartels were taking on political influence that was capable of threatening the stability of the entire region."

"That sounds serious, almost like the Communists trying to move in."

"Right, so, about two years ago, a number of us went to D.C. We met with the Director of National Intelligence, one step from the president."

"Why not the president?"

"When you hear what we proposed, you'll understand. What we proposed to the DNI was a war of our own. A war on the cartels, and we weren't proposing arrests and trials. We were proposing simply taking them out."

A.J. nodded. "Okay, now I see. What you suggested was patently illegal. Therefore, the White House needed plausible deniability if it all blew up."

"Exactly. So, the answer to your second question, the one about are we the good guys? I guess that answer is a little murky. I think morally the answer is yes. From a strictly legal sense, I suppose it's questionable. Before we go any further, do you have a problem with that?"

"What happens to me if I say I can't do this? I've been told 'my kind' only sees things in black or white."

"You'll still work for me. You'll be a DEA employee, probably in Bogotá doing intelligence analysis. A cushy, pretty well paying job. I wasn't going to let you get hung out to dry. I already knew a lot about you before you were even assigned to Cali. I asked for some Marines. I was given several jackets to look over. Yours intrigued me. The fact that I got to actually see you in action was an accident, but all it did was reinforce my instinct that I wanted you working for us."

A.J. nodded. She got out of her chair and walked to the large cooler built into the back wall of the cabin and fished out two Carta Blanca beers. She popped the bottle caps off with the remover screwed to the cooler and returned. She handed one to Tom and sat down. "This is the first opportunity I've had to mention something to you. When we were getting off the Pave Low in Cali, the crew chief told me a homing device had been detected in our group. Were you aware of that?"

"Yeah, he told me the same thing after your hearing. What does your brain tell you about what that was doing in our group?"

"Is this a test?" She smiled.

"Maybe, run with it. Tell me what you think."

"Okay, analytically, I know it wasn't me. The cowboys were using it to trail us, but they kept following you guys. Not me. So… the device was either on one of you or in our gear. Since the cowboys would have had no idea what gear we'd bring, it was on a person."

"So far, so good, A.J. Now, what does your gut tell you? Not your brain, your gut. Who was it?"

"It had to be Morris, Roberto, or you. My gut says Morris is too stupid to have done it deliberately. I'm still alive, so it wasn't you; ergo, it was Roberto."

"Excellent! I suspected him too. Add to that the fact that Roberto disappeared right after the mission. A fact you would have had no way of knowing. So, carrying this one step further, who was the target?"

A.J. thought a moment and stared into Tom's eyes, "You! You were the target. The rest of us were just gravy. You were who they wanted!"

He looked at her with a serious gaze. "I believe you're precisely correct. I've already told you more I've told than many of my other co-workers. We try to be compartmentalized. You already know things Isobel doesn't. By the same token, she knows a lot more than she's shared with you. There's a good reason for it. We are, to a large degree, on our own. We operate alone. What we do is actually quite dangerous if the wrong people get wind of it. If any of us are ever captured, the cartels won't hesitate to do whatever they feel necessary to interrogate us. And they are brutal beyond belief. So, before I go any further, are you in or not?"

A.J. had to think. This was exactly along the lines she had told T.D. and her mother what she felt her calling should be, but there was something nagging her. Something felt ever so slightly wrong. "I have one more question. My dad always said never to enter a room without an exit strategy. If I go in this room, how do I leave?"

"Great question. Any time you want out, you tell me. At that point, you would have two options. Stay on running a desk or go back to the good old USA and apply at any other government agency with a favorable letter of recommendation. You'd keep your G.S. rating, keep your time in grade, you'd lose nothing. Actually, I tend not to keep field people over a couple years. It's just simply too dangerous that someday the wrong person would recognize you."

"Okay, I guess I'm in," she replied, shaking his hand.

"Excellent. Later today, a package will be delivered to you at the hotel. There'll be some instructions for you as well as some passports and a fair amount of cash. You and Isobel will be staying a few more days. She'll brief you on your first job for us, and then you'll both be flying out. You may or may not ever see each other again."

A.J. turned and looked up on the bridge where Isobel was still keeping the captain and crew occupied. Her hand was on the deckhand's ass and her arm around the captain's neck. "She's quite friendly with the guys, isn't she, Tom? I think she's been testing me to see how far I'll go in that direction. True?"

"Yes, very true, but remember, I will never tell you to do anything sexual that feels wrong to you. I don't agree with that personally. If I need to get someone laid, I can hire any number of ladies with one phone call. Besides, after talking to Hendrix, I'm afraid if you ever felt I was taking advantage of you, Hendrix or your father would kill me, and if they didn't get the job done, your mother could subcontract it." He grinned.

He doesn't realize my mother is quite capable of doing the job herself if she feels the need. A.J. smiled back.

Suddenly the gold Penn Senator reel in front of Tom began singing as a large fish stripped line off the reel. "Fish on!" Tom yelled up to the bridge. The captain disentangled himself from Isobel, and the mate slid down the stainless ladder from the bridge and grabbed A.J.'s rod, winding in line as rapidly as possible to clear the deck for the job ahead. Tom climbed into the fighting chair, and the mate placed the singing rod's butt into the socket built into the chair.

Once the fish quit running, Tom began winding. He would pull the rod up and wind down, taking in line. Soon, the fish jumped, revealing its identity as a large sailfish. The crew was exited, and A.J. was too. It was the first time she had ever seen a fish that large, and the teamwork between the crew and the angler fascinated her. The captain backed down, putting the boat in reverse and backing toward the fish to give Tom an opportunity to get some line back.

A.J. did what seemed the wisest move; she got out of the way. Isobel was still on the bridge, but other than occasionally encouraging Tom, she stayed out of the way too. Fifteen minutes later, the fish was at the boat. The deckhand grabbed the leader, and the captain kicked the twin diesels into neutral and dropped down to the deck to help. They pulled the fish on board and held it up as Isobel took photos from the bridge.

"Señor Tom, do you wish to keep the fish or let him go?"

Tom thought briefly and answered, "Put him back. Let him swim again. We have pictures. Let's get back to trolling. We have dorado left to catch!"

The crew returned the fish to the blue water, and Isobel came down to the deck. The mate re-rigged the lines, putting out three dorado rigs, each with a teaser and a ballyhoo. In no time at all, they were hooked up. In the next hour the three landed six beautiful dorado. The captain indicated it was time to head in. The daily thunderstorms would be starting up soon.

A.J. looked down at her outfit. Her shorts as well as her stomach and legs were covered with blood. The dorado had been real bleeders. "Shit, I've got to get this off." She grabbed the water hose and began washing off. Isobel and Tom were covered too. She and Isobel peeled out of their shorts, leaving them in just their bikinis.

"Señor Tom," the captain called, "we run up the sailfish flag, no?" He was holding a blue flag with a white sailfish on it.

"Sí, Captain, run up the flag!" Tom answered, taking a big swig out of a beer. He grabbed two more and handed one to each of the girls.

A.J. thought for a moment and, displaying a devilish grin, pulled off her top. "Here, Captain, run this up the flag too!" She tossed her bikini top up to the bridge.

Isobel looked at her in shock. "Why, you little slut! Hold on, Captain, fly this flag too!" she yelled, peeling her top off as well. The girls laughed as the captain and mate tied the tops to the line and ran them up the little flag line. It was difficult for them to do it and stare at the boobs too.

"What was that all about, A.J.?" Tom asked.

"Well, Isobel has been telling me I need to improve my people skills. I just thought the crew would get a kick out of it. I know I am, besides, I thought the girls could use a little sun!" She was grinning ear to ear.

"What are you planning on doing when we get to the marina?"

"Tom, I've got a tee shirt in my bag in the cabin. Now, since we're just riding now, let's get down to important shit. Like drinking!"

A.J. and Isobel sat down in their chairs and turned up their beers. Tom did the intelligent thing. He sat on the stern and alternated between staring at the girls and winking at the crew.

An hour later, the boat was backing into the dock. The girls were more properly attired now; they had put on tee shirts and jeans. There was no hiding the fact that they were braless, but they were dressed. Two men met them at the dock.

A.J. leaned to Tom and asked, "Who are they?"

"It's okay; they're my bodyguards. The captain is going to deliver the fish to a restaurant, and we'll all go there tonight and eat our own fish. We'll give you a ride back to your hotel."

One of Tom's bodyguards took Isobel's camera and snapped several photos of the three fishermen and the crew with their fish on the board behind them. Tom and the girls then loaded up in the Toyota Land Cruiser with the two bodyguards and sped off toward the Fiesta Americana.

Chapter 13

Puerto Vallarta, Mexico

"So, Anna, are you ready for your brief on your first job?"

"Yep, ready to go. By the way, are your boobs burnt too?"

"A little, I still can't believe you, of all people, would pull a stunt like that."

"I know, me either. I wanted to do something outside my comfort zone, and like I told Tom, you've been after me to improve my people skills, so…"

"Well, I don't know if stripping qualifies as a people skill, but you definitely got out of your comfort zone. Back to work, dear. Your first assignment is going to be a 'snatch & grab.'"

A what?"

"A 'snatch & grab' is shorthand for a kidnapping. The intelligence nerds will have identified someone who is supposed to have information we consider valuable. So, basically, we snatch 'em, and then other people will carry them to a secure location and interrogate them until we get what we want."

"What happens to them then?"

"It's best you and I don't know. Sometimes they might be turned as a double agent. Sometimes they might get shipped out of their home country and set up with a new identity, sometimes, well, sometimes their body is dumped in a public place as a warning. I think, if possible, we try to make it look like another cartel actually did the dirty work."

"So how do we come in? I mean, why a woman?"

"Because it's easier for a woman to catch them with their guard down."

"Their guard or their pants?"

"Good one, A.J. Yeah, sometimes their pants. But if we're going that direction, we would usually use a hooker. Problem with that is if the mark knows he's gonna get laid, he's usually going to take them somewhere he's comfortable. That means somewhere he has guards. That means a bigger team, shooting, it gets complicated. Your job, and mine, is to maneuver the mark to a pre-set location. Then we can bring in the snatch team. The rest of our team snatches both of us, puts us in a van, and speeds away into the night. Later we get dropped off, and the mark goes to his interrogation team."

"So what's to stop one of them from just snatching us?"

"Location. You or I would approach the mark in a public place. We have backup. It's not that it's impossible, but we're pretty good at avoiding that. The good thing is if you get that feeling, you know, if you smell it going south, you just leave. Or there will be signal to give your backup. I've done that a couple times."

A.J. sat. She was pondering what Isobel had told her. It was generic, an overview. She wanted more. "That's okay as far as it goes. What about the mechanics? How do you actually make the kill? Speaking metaphorically of course."

"Oh, well, in a way that's the easiest part. You would do a stalk; you would determine a club or other location where it'll be dark and noisy. It has to be public, of course, for you and your backup to be able to get in. Once you get him, or her, more or less alone, I usually drug them. I use liquid Xanax. By itself, it doesn't have a massive effect, but combined with alcohol, it turns one drink into eleven. If the target is hopped up on coke, which is frequently the case, it might take two doses. Then, you help them stagger to the door. If it goes great, you'll get in a cab with him that we control, and you're home free. If he's a major player, he'll want his limo and bodyguards; that's where it gets hairy."

"Yeah, I can see that. You'd be outnumbered, even with backup. Would you usually abort then?"

"I always have. I have them drop me somewhere. If they think they're going to get me somewhere for the night, I fake being too drunk. I've even had to puke in the car. That got me slapped around by the disappointed bodyguards and thrown out at the next corner, but it got me away from them."

"Okay, Isobel, I think I've got snatch & grab. Do you have the details? The where, who, and when?"

"Nope, that's the beauty of it. Tom will contact you once you get to your destination. What I don't know, I can't give up."

"Have you ever done any wet work?"

"No. I think I could, but I've never been asked. I'm pretty sure I've done some recon that turned into a car bombing or a kill, but I don't know it for a fact. I have a feeling you may wind up getting that added to your job description, but that's pure speculation on my part. You're strange; sometimes you're as cold as ice, no bullshit, no remorse. Then you shock the shit out of me by peeling off your panties in the ladies room or going topless and laughing about it."

"You're right, I'm an enigma even to myself. I can compartmentalize major parts of my emotions. I don't really understand it, but the no remorse part? Trust me, that has good and bad sides to it. It makes it very, very difficult to have any proper sense of affection toward people."

Isobel stared at A.J. She looked into her eyes. She saw a cool, emotionless, and almost vacant look. She had seen it before. Unfortunately, the people who had exhibited that look before were bad men. Very, very bad men. "I saw you got your package from Mr. Tom last night. Was I right about needing some wigs?" Isobel decided to change the subject; she wasn't really comfortable with where the conversation had been going.

"I guess, I've got several passports where I'm a blond, and even a redhead, so I guess I'll need some wigs. I like my hair just as it is, but the practical side of me says short hair is so uncommon in this part of the world, I'd stand out. I need to blend in, right?"

"Absolutely. So, let's get dressed and head out shopping! You'll be leaving soon, so we'll need to pick up some luggage for you as well."

"Can we get some more casual clothes too, Isobel? I get it about the sexy stuff, but I only have a few jeans and a few tops that don't look like they came from Frederick's of Hollywood. I don't know, but I have a feeling I won't need the 'hooker look' on a continuous basis!"

Isobel laughed, "That's fine. Look around while we're in town today. We'll see what the other señoritas your age wear, and again, we need you blending. It's your camouflage, no?"

"Yeah, I guess. My concept of camo is going to have to be expanded I guess. I've got to get back to running too! I'll bet I've gained five pounds. In fact, before we get ready to go today, I'm heading for the beach. I'm not sure I want to run in town, but I'm comfy on the beach. Wanna come?"

"Sure, I'll give it a try. I want to see how a badass Marine compares to a college track star anyway!"

An hour later, Isobel knew the difference. She could take A.J. in a sprint, not by a lot, but she could take her. Where A.J. murdered her was just flat-out running with no break. A.J. told Isobel it made a difference when you were used to running with a twenty- or thirty-kilo pack.

"Okay, you win. I should've known better than to challenge you on that one."

"Damned right, just like I won't challenge you on how long it takes for you to have a man wrapped around your finger. I've got a lot to learn there."

"True, but you can shorten the time required by removing clothing, and you've proven a reasonable talent for that!"

"I plead guilty, but like I said, I'm still trying to expand my limits. Those were experiments. They might or might not ever be repeated!"

The two spent another day shopping. When they returned to the hotel, there was an envelope for Anna at the desk. She waited until she got to the room to open it. There was a note and airline tickets. She turned to Isobel, "I guess the vacation's over, Isobel. I leave on the 11:00 a.m. flight out."

"Where are you going, Anna?"

"Can't tell you, or anyone else. I guess this is it. Can you help me pack?"

"Sure. Wanna go to the lounge tonight, maybe see Enrique again?"

A.J. laughed out loud. "Oh dear God no, he was such a loser. It was kind of fun to kick him in the balls, in a figurative sense of course."

"Would you have been above doing it in a literal sense?"

"Hell no, if the situation called for it, I could cut them off. I'd just have to have a *really* good reason."

Isobel looked at A.J. for a long time. "The scary thing is I believe you."

"And so you should, Isobel. So you should."

Chapter 14

Cartagena, Colombia

A.J. collected her things and headed for the cabin door on the LAN Airline MD-80. She had flown in from Miami again. She held a new identity on her passport, new blond hair on her head, and new heels on her feet.

Damn Isobel and these shoes!

She'd kicked them off during the flight. While being willing to face the fact that they were a needed part of her new identity, it didn't mean she had to like them! She made her way through customs and baggage claim and headed to the arrival area after clearing immigration.

Just as she had been told, there was a man holding a sign saying "DeJesus." She walked to him with the cart containing her luggage and stated, "I'm DeJesus," in Spanish. He nodded and simply said, "Come with me please."

God, this is so much easier than the back and forth shit!

She followed him to a Volkswagen mini van. He delivered her to a rather ordinary apartment in a mundane building. She tipped the driver with an amount he seemed satisfied with. Once inside she noted that it was furnished in a contemporary fashion with definite Colombian influence. She noted upon entering that even though the building was hardly extravagant, it was reasonably secure, requiring key card entrance to the building and the elevator. Her door seemed heavy, indicating it was possibly reinforced in some way, and it had a deadbolt.

The instructions she'd committed to memory indicated she would have a visitor in the morning. Anna saw no need in locking herself in her room, plus she was hungry. She threw on jeans and sneakers. A stylish hat and scarf completed the look. She looked in the mirror and thought she vaguely resembled a Hollywood starlet out on a stroll attempting to avoid the paparazzi. She had no idea who could possibly be interested in her arrival in Cartagena, but she would be disguised nonetheless. She was on a mission. If possible, she needed to locate pizza, a marketplace, a restaurant, and possibly a bar. In that order. Her search was successful, and after a pleasant dinner, a few hours later she considered herself moved in. She turned on the television and was mildly surprised that nothing of significance had changed since she'd left Colombia several weeks ago.

A.J. awoke to the buzzing of her intercom, someone was at the door downstairs. She staggered from the couch toward the intercom, trying to shake the cobwebs out. *God, what time is it?* She glanced at her stainless Seiko diver's watch and was shocked to see it was nearly 0900 hours.

"Yes?" she yelled into the intercom.

"Anna, are you okay?" an unfamiliar voice asked. "It's Manuel and Maria, can we come up?"

"Sure." She pressed the button and heard the buzz that indicated the lock was released.

At least the names matched what Tom had provided in her envelope. A.J. didn't remember falling asleep on the sofa. She must have really been exhausted. She ran to the bathroom and looked in the mirror. Oh well, she had seen worse looking back at her. There was barely enough time for a quick job with the toothbrush before the doorbell rang. She looked through the peephole; Manuel and Maria matched their photos.

A.J. opened the deadbolt and asked the two in. Manuel and Maria were definitely Colombian; A.J. would be willing to bet a pretty large amount of money they weren't really named Manuel and Maria, but they definitely looked like a cute, young Colombian couple.

"Anna, are we too early?"

"No, no, it's not your fault. I got in yesterday, moved in, and then I went looking for some dinner. I found a little place around the corner, had dinner and some wine, and the next thing I knew, I was on the couch listening to the intercom buzzing. Definitely not your fault!"

"Well, as Mr. Tom may have explained, for the time being, we will be your handlers. We'll also be training you, walking you through the fine points of a snatch and grab. We'll also be doing a lot of trial runs with the rest of our team. The more we've all worked together, the better we will do, no?" Manuel had delivered the speech. Maria smiled at A.J.

"Of course, I'm sure I could use a lot of practice at kidnapping. We actually do cover it in training in the Corps, but it's a more violent, less subtle method. Lots of shooting!"

Maria jumped in. "Ah, speaking of shooting, we have some items for you." She had been carrying a lady's briefcase; it looked like alligator or caiman skin. She placed it on the table in front of the couch. "We brought you some items you may need." She opened the case. There were some files and papers inside; she picked them out, setting them on the coffee table. "As you can see, there is a false bottom in the case," she explained, lifting the bottom up to expose two guns. Each had two spare magazines and a suppressor. One was a .22 caliber High Standard automatic; the other was a Beretta nine mm. She picked up the nine.

"I love this gun. My dad has one just like it; it's what I learned to shoot on. What's the .22 for?"

"Anna, sometimes you'll be wearing clothing and carrying a purse that won't allow you to disguise the Beretta. In fact, we also have a two-shot Derringer you can hide almost anywhere." Maria winked. "As you're probably aware, the .22 is only to get you out of a jam or to do a hit. A hit with the .22 has to be at arm's length, two or more shots to the head, preferably right behind the ear. We'll go to lunch together, and then we'll begin your training. We have a warehouse we use for rehearsals. We've got a simulated bar inside. We'll take you and start your training."

"Yes, let me get a shower. How should I dress?"

"Jeans are okay for today, Anna. We'll graduate to full-dress rehearsals later," Manuel answered.

Twenty minutes later, A.J. came out and announced, "I'm ready!"

She'd thought she was ready. A week of practice later, she was very unsure. She had "drugged" and helped kidnap every male member of the team, as well as Maria and another female member of the team. The hardest thing to learn was faking the sex appeal. It wasn't an issue of the sex itself—A.J. was hardly a virgin. She considered sex to be healthy entertainment and cardio, but nothing to have any lasting concerns about. It was the feigned affection and attraction she had to learn. Manuel and Maria had finally pronounced A.J. as "operational," but not without reservations.

"Anna, you're almost flawless with the operational components. Your decision-making skills are as good or better as any I've seen."

"I'm assuming there's a "but" coming here somewhere, Manuel."

Maria laughed as she took the lead. "Actually, the butt is what's missing! You've got to get a little better at acting slutty. You're getting better, but half of distracting these marks is making their little head take over control of their big head. You've got to accidently let their arm brush your boob and toss your butt around a little more when you get up to go to the ladies room."

"I know, I know, I understand the concept. It's all quite foreign for me. I've had a lot of male friends, but I've never had a guy I felt like chasing. Fast walking maybe, chasing? No."

"We understand," Manuel continued. "You are probably going to be exactly what we need for wet work. Cold, calculating, no remorse. But to get the intel we need to decide the who, when, and where to make a hit, we have to get these individuals to our interrogators. These snatches using a sexy girl as bait works really well. We can't trust hookers to be motivated. Their loyalty is to the money; ours is to the cause. We're going to do a couple ops with you and Maria working together. We're starting in the next few days. Maria has the bios and photos of the marks, where they hang out. You two work together. Make a few dry runs to get the mark interested. Show him the bait. Then we'll put the team together."

It did come together. Over the next three weeks, A.J. and Maria had trolled and hooked two fairly low-level cartel members, placing them in the hands of the interrogation team. Manuel and Maria had given her good grades.

"Anna, you've improved. Your acting skills have improved. In fact, on our last gig, you were making me hot. The mark never had a chance. If the Xanax hadn't hit him, he was going to need some relief, immediately!" The girls both giggled a little.

"We have a special mission for you." Manuel looked serious as he sat on A.J.'s couch. "On your last trip to the Python Bar, an important mark saw you. He's put out word he wants to sleep with the blonde bitch from Miami. He's a big player; it would be a major coup to pick his brain. We have to have him. His name is Carlos the Scorpion; at least that's his street name. Are you up for it?"

"Sure, we can do it."

"That's the thing. He's telling his bodyguards not to let two women anywhere near him. Word is out about you two. Several players have gone missing after being seen with the two of you. We've got to change the plan somewhat. You'll still have backup, but you'll have to take him alone."

"How would it work if we do a trial run? I'll troll the bar, if possible have a conversation with Señor Scorpion, and then have to leave for a date. Maybe he'll be a little off his game second time around. Think it would work?"

Maria and Manuel looked at each other and nodded. "Yes, we'll try it your way. It sounds like a good plan. We will still have your back."

Two nights later, A.J. walked out of the Python feeling it had gone well. Manuel had gone in and scoped out the bar. He had seen Carlos and his entourage enter about 2300. He left and signaled A.J. that the target was in the bar. She sat at the bar a half hour before one of Carlos's bodyguards had approached her asking if she would like to join his employer at his table.

She left an hour later. After several drinks, a dance, and giving him a peck on the cheek, she had told him she was feeling a little sick. She had asked him if she could return the next night for a real kiss, and perhaps more. He had enthusiastically agreed.

The following evening, she and her team returned. Shortly after midnight, many drinks and two doses of Xanax later, she was helping Carlos out the door, bodyguards and all, looking for the cab with her snatch team inside.

Then the wheels began to fall off.

Chapter 15

Python Bar

Cartagena, Columbia

A.J. started out the door with The Scorpion, his entourage in tow. She'd spotted the cab and headed for it when a large bodyguard blocked her and waved up a black Suburban. *Shit, Plan B I guess*. A.J. hesitated at the door, turning to the bodyguard. "I think I'll just get a cab and go home."

"Get in the truck, señorita," he said gruffly. "Señor Scorpion plans to see you in his bed when he wakes up. We wouldn't want to disappoint him, would we?"

"No, of course not," A.J. replied. Scorpion, A.J., and one bodyguard got in the back; the big bodyguard climbed in the front with the driver. The Suburban pulled away from the bar rapidly. A.J. resisted the urge to look behind her to see if the cab was following with the remainder of her team shadowing them. "Where are we going?"

“Why to meet Señor Scorpion, Señorita DeJesus. Wasn’t that your ambition tonight?” She looked at the nearly unconscious man beside her. The surprise on her face had to be obvious. “I’m afraid tonight there will be a change in your plans. The man next to you is our employer’s brother. You see tonight, you were the ‘mark’ as you call it. We made you and your team.” His phone rang. “Sí?” he answered. He listened for a few moments, replied, “Well done,” and snapped the Motorola flip phone shut. “Yes, señorita, as I was saying, we made you and your team. We aren’t as stupid as you and your DEA friends think. Right after we pulled away, two of our men opened up on the cab, killing three of your friends; then with all the confusion, it was a simple task to put a large knife into your escort’s kidney. He should have bled out by now, wouldn’t you say?”

A.J. felt a moment of blinding anger, but it was quickly replaced by a wave of determination and accompanying calm. “So, what are Señor Scorpion’s plans for me?”

The big man laughed. “We already discussed that, Señorita DeJesus. We are taking you to him. You will wake up in his bed, assuming you get any sleep. We have some people who want to interrogate you, señorita. Our instructions are to deliver you unharmed. Of course, there’s no reason we couldn’t have some fun before we arrive. Don’t you agree?”

That was when she heard the bodyguard next to her, the skinnier one, undoing his zipper. “You know what to do.” He grinned.

A.J. turned to him to watch as he unbuckled his belt. She saw exactly what she was hoping for, what looked like a Colt .357 revolver in his belt. She decided it was now or never to go to Plan C.

"Of course." She smiled. "May I have my purse please?" she asked, turning to the big man in the front seat.

"Certainly, señorita, you realize I've already removed your cute little pistol."

"I would have expected no less, señor, I just wanted my lip-gloss."

The big man handed her the tube of lip-gloss. She applied it generously and seductively, glancing from one man to another as she licked her lips. She turned to the man in front and pulled up her dress. She started to remove her thong.

"No need for that, señorita, you can do what we had in mind with your present clothing."

"Think of these as a trophy for you, señor." *And a distraction.* She tossed her thong toward his face in the front seat; her timing and execution had to be perfect from here on out. She twisted in her seat and moved her left hand and her head toward his lap. In a fraction of a second she became the aggressor. She head-butted the man in the back seat as the man in the front tried to remove her panties from his face. Blood sprayed from skinny guard's nose, and at the same time, her right hand went to the Colt. She pivoted toward the front seat. Two quick explosions rocked the car as the 140-grain bullets penetrated big guard in the front's head; blood and brain spattered the windshield and bulletproof glass in the side window. A second later the muzzle was under skinny man's chin, and another explosion went off. The top of his head impacted the roof. *Always two in the head with a pistol* her dad had told her, but it was obvious one would do in this case.

As the driver's head turned toward her, he felt the muzzle contact his head right behind his ear.

“Do exactly as I say and you’ll live, “she told him. Her voice seemed quiet and calm to her. Was it the fact that her ears had been assaulted by the shots in the closed car or just the incredible feeling of calm? The driver nodded. “Stop the car, put it in park, and get out. Don’t even think about taking the keys. Leave the door open and stand right by the car.” As he exited, she climbed to the front. The driver took his chance and ran toward the back of the Suburban.

She exited the car and took careful aim. Her first shot hit him in the back of his right thigh. She calmly walked up to him. “I told you I’d let you live. I want you to take a message to Señor Scorpion. There was no need to kill my friends. If Scorpion wants a war, a war he shall have. I am pissed. He has no idea what I am capable of. I will be coming for him. First, I will kill his men then his mistresses then his wife and then his children. Do you understand?”

The man nodded in pain and in fear. She could see the dark stain in his crotch where he had pissed himself. “One more thing. You tell The Scorpion that if he ever wakes up with me in his bed, he better check to see if his cajones are still attached. Now, take your gun out and slide it this way.” He did. She picked it up and carefully backed toward the Suburban then hopped inside and drove away.

She had no idea where she was, but she began to head back in what she thought was the general direction of the club district. She turned the rearview mirror so she could see the “mark”, the man they had thought was the Scorpion. *He has to be totally unconscious to have slept through this!* So, now he was the brother. So be it, he could still have value. She crossed Calle 35 and had an idea where she was, but when she went by the Parque del

Centenario, she knew exactly where she was. She reached over to grab the big guard's cell and called Manuel's cell number. He answered on the first ring.

"Hello?"

"Manuel, it's DeJesus. I need help."

"Anna, are you okay? It all went to shit. We have four dead, and you were missing. We all assumed the worst. Where are you?"

"I'm driving around in a black Suburban that isn't mine, and I have two dead bodies and Scorpion's brother drugged in the back. I'm near Parque del Centenario. How soon can you have someone here? I damned sure don't want to be pulled over."

"There's an alley on the west side of the park. That would be away from the ocean. Cruise around there. Don't park. Whose phone are you on?"

"One of the bodyguards."

"Okay, hang up and take the battery out. We'll be in a taxi and a white Ford van, ten minutes, tops. Bye."

He was accurate. Nine minutes later, she passed a taxi with a white van trailing. She immediately pulled over and shut the truck off. It stunk to high heaven in the Suburban. The coppery smell of blood was everywhere; the smell of gunpowder was nearly overwhelmed by the odor of someone's bowels having emptied. She looked in the mirror; she was a sight. Blood was spattered all over her face and her right arm. *At least it isn't mine*. She stepped out of the Suburban as soon as Manuel ran to the door. Maria was right behind him. Two men with what looked like MAC 10s had taken up positions in front and behind the train of vehicles. Men were coming out of the van with a stretcher. One looked extremely out of place. He had to be sixty. He was short, bald, and definitely an American.

His clothing resembled someone who had walked off a 1930's safari movie set.

Manuel looked into the Suburban. "My God. Did you do all this?"

A.J. nodded. "Plus one more that I let go with a round in his leg. By the way, the guy in the back seat isn't Carlos. They were onto us; but supposedly, the mark is Scorpions' brother made up to look like him. I was the target. We've been blown."

Manuel nodded. "I agree, get in the cab." Maria put her arm around A.J.

"I take it vomiting didn't work?" she asked A.J., making a nervous attempt at humor.

"Not even close. They were onto me from the beginning." She glanced into the front seat as they got into the taxi. A.J. could see the driver had a MAC 10 in his lap.

"Anna, you're covered in blood. Are you sure you're okay?"

"I'm fine, Maria, just fucking fine." A.J. watched Manuel as he crawled around the interior of the Suburban; he seemed to be gathering and placing items in a baggy. He was also wiping down the interior. Maria got out of the taxi and ran back to the van, returning with a wad of gauze and a bottle of water.

Manuel climbed in the front seat, and Maria returned to the back and began wiping A.J.'s face and arms. A.J. pulled off her blonde wig. Manuel handed A.J. her panties. "I have to ask, why were your panties in the front seat?"

"I tossed them to the big bodyguard to distract him for a second."

"The panties, what caliber are they? They did a number on his head."

“. 357 I think. They did the job. I grabbed the gun of the guard next to me and took them out.”

“Yeah, I saw that. I also saw the guard in the back had his zipper down and his thing out.”

“Yeah, I think he was expecting a mind-blowing orgasm, so I gave him one. Like I said, I left the driver with a message for the Scorpion. I said I was coming after him, and if he wanted a war, I would bring him one. I threatened to kill his men, mistresses, wife, and children. Was I too extreme? I mean, seriously, there was no need to kill our team. That pissed me off, but if you or Tom tell me I was wrong…”

“I'll speak to Tom, but I think you did fine. Remember, in this part of the world, you need to make it personal. They understand it. By the way, here.”

He had handed A.J. a box of playing cards. She opened it with a question mark on her face. Each card was a queen of spades. “Huh?”

“It was Tom's idea. It's your calling card. Story is during World War Two and Vietnam; some special U.S. troops had a habit of leaving an ace of spades in the mouths of dead enemy soldiers. Tom thought you should personalize your kills. Being a woman, he thought the queen would be more appropriate. I left one in the mouths of your two friends.” Manuel put the cards in A.J.'s purse and handed it to her. “I've got your two-shot derringer in the bag here, along with their cell phones.”

“Where are we going?”

Maria answered, “Our place. You are staying with Manuel and me. We'll have some discreet guards in place too. You need to lay low a few days. We'll arrange the move.”

A.J. nodded and sat back in the taxi. It was only a few hours until dawn. She had never seen Manuel's place. It was a small, walled estate home in the city. Maria escorted A.J. to a bedroom and showed her the shower. "I'll get you a tee shirt and some panties, Anna. Is there anything else you need?"

"Yes there is. Does Manuel have any Jack Daniel's?"

"I'm sure he does. I'll bring the bottle."

A.J. nodded. She showered, and when she came out in a towel, Maria handed her a tee shirt and undies. She dropped the towel and put them on. She looked out the glass doors and saw a small patio up against the three-meter high concrete wall. She went to her purse and pulled out her zippo. Maria handed her the bottle of Jack and a glass.

"Do you want me to sit with you?"

"Have you got a cigarette?"

"Sure, let's go outside." Maria watched A.J. as she sat, smoking the cigarette and holding the zippo. Her thumb was lightly rubbing back and forth on some dark smudges. Her hands were shaking ever so slightly as she worked on the Jack. "Wanna talk about it?"

"Have you ever killed anyone, Maria?"

"No, I haven't."

"Then no offense, but no."

Maria sat with A.J. until the gray light of dawn began to appear in the part of the sky visible over the wall. A.J.'s hands had stopped shaking; the bottle of Jack was half empty. Her eyes were closed. Maria quietly rose and left the patio.

Chapter 16

Cartagena, Colombia

A.J. woke in a strange bed with a splitting headache. She thought for a few moments, and it all came flooding back into her brain. Sadness, anger, but the brief flutter of emotions vanished as they always did. She had been placed in a bad situation, and she'd done what had to be done to resolve it. It was as simple as that. No regrets, they were not allowed to interfere.

She carefully moved to a sitting position. She looked around; it was light outside. Her bedroom was pleasant with various shades of white in differing textures—cotton, muslin, wool, and carpet. It had stucco walls and bleached white beams overhead. It was very hard to tell if the house was a hundred years old or a clever re-creation. A white ceiling fan whirred silently overhead. She saw Maria had left a glass of water and some aspirin on the bedside table. A.J. smelled food, bacon, eggs maybe? Since the smell didn't provoke any nausea, she assumed she would survive. In the bath, she found a new toothbrush and some jeans.

A few moments later, she wandered down the hall to find Manuel and Maria seated at the bar. Their cook was placing more food into dishes lined up on the bar. Fruit, juices, food, and coffee. Coffee! That was it, breakfast of champions. There was a reason Colombian coffee was widely considered the worlds best.

"Good morning, how's the head?" Maria asked.

"God, Maria. Please, not so loud! What time is it?"

Manuel and Maria both laughed. "It's a little after eleven. If you need some clothes…"

A.J. looked down and realized he was hinting. She seemed to be missing her bra this morning, and her high beams were definitely on. "Oh, sorry Manuel, I didn't think about that."

"Oh, don't be, dear, he's enjoying the view, I can promise you." Maria laughed. "Come, eat a little something to absorb any leftover Jack Daniel's. We're going to move you. We've decided to re-examine our security. We thought it was pretty tight, but obviously there are some problems."

"Yeah, I was thinking the same thing last night. Once it was apparent they were going to interrogate me, among other things, I was glad I knew so little. I knew your cell number, Manuel, but as far as where you lived, or even your real names, I didn't have a clue. Would have sucked for me, but I couldn't have done much damage. By the way, this is a kick-ass house."

"It's rented. Some cowboy had it until he wound up with a slit throat," Manuel answered.

Just as A.J. began to put food on her plate, the power blinked in the kitchen. The TV went off. A split second later, a small shock could be felt in the floor, and a few seconds later, the low, bass rumble got there along with the minor pressure change. A.J. recognized it instantly as a large quantity of explosives going off, maybe a kilometer or so away.

"Sounds like a car bomb," Manuel speculated. He picked up his cell. Maria grabbed A.J.'s arm and pulled her down the hall to her closet.

A.J. picked out some of Marie's clothes for a couple days as well as some toiletries from Maria's things; the rest could wait. When they walked through the kitchen, Manuel looked very serious.

"It was a truck bomb, a big one, right in front of your apartment building. The building is basically gone; there are many killed and injured. It tells us several things. We have definite security issues, your message got to The Scorpion, and we are at war. I need to call Señor Tom, but I'll use the sat phone."

"Oh, Anna, thank God we decided to bring you here last night."

A.J. nodded. Manuel had gone in the other room. She looked at Maria. "It may tell us something else. Last night, they knew I was Anna DeJesus, and apparently, they knew where I lived. If we can determine who else knew that, it would narrow down where our security leaks are. Something else, please ask Manuel if I could speak to Tom. Don't be offended, but I need to tell Tom some things that the two of you don't need to know, just in case. I trust you two, but I don't know everyone you interact with. Ask Tom if I can use the sat phone in private, okay? Please do it Maria, now!"

"Hello, A.J." Tom's voice came through the sat phone in a strange, slightly distorted tone. It sounded a little alien, but the good news was it couldn't be traced or tapped unless you were connected with the U.S. or Soviet intelligence services.

"Hello, I'm sorry I started such a shitstorm."

"Don't be. It really started while you were still a Marine. We've had a few cocaine crime bosses that have taken a violent position with the DEA. Hell, they've even assassinated their own judges and politicians; I guess we shouldn't feel like the Lone Ranger."

"There's a couple things I called about, and they're not connected. First, if you can swing it, I think we need to get T.D. involved. We can apply some logic to where we think the leaks could be, but T.D.'s people can add telephone and electronic intercept data to it. Think you could call him and tell him his sister needs him?"

"Sure, I'll get the ball rolling. What's the other item?"

"Tattoos."

"What, you want my opinion on where to have one done?"

"No. Tom, I'm having a fucking hard time seeing humor in any of this." She was standing now, nearly shouting into the phone. "After I've just had the blood and brains of two people on my face in one night and innocent people lost their lives just because some testosterone-filled jerk wanted me dead. The two goons that were in the car with me had tattoos of a scorpion on the inside of their left wrist. I'm not positive, but I'm almost sure I saw one Roberto that night we had to get the helo to pick us up. Know anything about that?"

"I'm sorry. I wasn't making light of what you went through. I was trying to introduce some gallows humor. Sorry, girl. As far as the tattoos, actually, yeah. We didn't know at the time, but we're putting it together. Although that tattoo is fairly popular anyway in Central and South America, Carlos seems to have adopted it as a calling card of his inner circle. Here's what you do need to know. Roberto has dropped off the face of the earth. We're positive he was a mole, feeding intelligence either to Scorpion or anyone willing to pay him. He seems to have hooked up with Carlos. As you may have guessed, Roberto hates your guts; and now you've insulted Scorpion's honor as well, so both of them want you very dead."

"That can be a good thing though, can't it?"

Tom laughed. "Okay, A.J., tell me why it's a good thing people want you dead."

"Because they're allowing their decisions, their actions, to be impacted by their emotions, not reason."

"That's why you amaze me. Here you are, what, twenty-three? You see right through what a normal person couldn't get past. Most people would say a life-or-death decision always is colored by emotion; you say emotion has no place in the decision. By the way, Manuel tells me you did a hell of a job last night. I knew you could take 'em out long distance. Didn't know you could take them down sitting next to them."

"Well, it's certainly different, I can say that. The decision to actually pull the trigger is easier when you're sitting next to the threat. Tom, what are we gonna do? We're in a war!"

"You're right. I'll have to go above my pay grade for approval, but I think I'm going to green light going all out. We'll turn the Queen of Spades loose, and you're not our only wet-work asset. You were right what you told Scorpion's driver that if he wants a war he shall have one. Get some rest and get ready; Manuel will let you know. By the way, it was a good call not letting Manuel or Maria hear this. We need 100 percent compartmentalization from here on out. Anything else?”

“No, just remember, let’s get T.D. involved, the sooner, the better.”

“Copy, See you soon.” The line beeped with the loss-of-signal tone.

Chapter 17

Cartagena, Colombia

"Well, it certainly looks like there are changes coming; you can feel it in the wind. They've gone too far this time. I have a feeling we're going to turn the hounds of hell loose on them."

"Are you calling me a hound, a bitch? I'm a queen, remember?"

"Why, Anna, there is a sense of humor in there! Yes, Señorita DeJesus, you are a queen: The Queen of Spades. You will be an amazing weapon. There's no need now to try to make our actions look like that of a rival cartel."

A.J. leaned back in her chair; she and Manuel were in the office in his home. Each sat in a leather chair, very modern, South American contemporary designed chairs. Manuel had a desk, bookcases on two walls, and his pride and joy, a billiard table. "Tell me, I have some questions about the other night. If everyone thought the Scorpion was so dangerous, what in the hell were you thinking sending me in there alone?"

"I will tell you the truth, but you will not like it. The truth is we had calculated a 66 percent chance there would be a favorable outcome. You might pull off the snatch, you might wind up killing Scorpion, or he might wind up killing you. What actually happened was not anticipated, but it was still a satisfactory outcome. We are still interrogating Señor Scorpion's brother, and we have him as a possible exchange should one of our own be captured."

"Sixty-six percent, huh? I suppose those were acceptable odds for a combat operation; far less than ideal, but acceptable."

"I thought you would be angry!"

"Why? Many military operations have been undertaken with worse odds; I was told once I am an asset. Assets are to be utilized, and they are expendable. Or they can be used to acquire more assets, so, no Manuel, I'm not angry. Anger is something I don't understand. It's not that I've got some amazing self-control; it's my brain. I'm wired funny. I don't usually feel anger as anything but a fleeting feeling. Problem is it's the same way with friendship, love. All my emotions are sort of crippled.

"You said the interrogation was going well. Someone told me I probably didn't want to know how these are conducted, but actually I do. I was taught interrogation in the military, and the current thinking is violence and barbarism is not required or terribly effective. So, what can you tell me?"

"Do you remember seeing an old man in the van the night we picked you up?"

"Yes. He looked like he'd walked off a *Tarzan* movie set."

"Yes, that's him. We call him Dr. Dave. He's actually retired CIA. Story is he had gone over to the dark side. He was caught but couldn't be tried because of some kind of national security reasons. Instead, he was basically under house arrest for years, but he still worked for the Agency. Now he works for us. He uses a combination of drugs and hypnosis. The story goes, given enough time, he can take you back until you…"

"Remember when you were born, yes, I've heard the stories. Firsthand from my parents, as a matter of fact."

"They know Dr. Dave?"

"I'm absolutely sure. My brother and I have never been able to work out the particulars."

"Wow! From what I've been told, if you two can't work it out, it's way beyond secret; it's deep black shit!"

A.J. simply nodded.

There was a knock on Manuel's office door.

"Come."

It was Maria. She was holding a manila envelope. "Manuel, FedEx just delivered this. I'm assuming its orders. Shall we open it?"

Apparently with approval from higher up, Tom had indeed turned loose the hounds of hell. Over the next two weeks, there were numerous deaths within the ranks of the cartels in Cartagena. A.J. was only directly involved in one; she had no direct knowledge of the others for security reasons, but she was very aware they were happening.

Hers had taken place in a lounge. Manuel had done an excellent job planning it. He had given A.J. numerous photos of the target. His name was Rico, and intelligence indicated he was a lieutenant of Carlos the Scorpion. In several of the photographs, there were hints of the scorpion tattoo on his arm.

The plan itself had been comparatively simple. A.J.'s training and experience had shown her the simpler the plan, the higher the likelihood for success. Once Manuel's inexpensive paid lookouts had reported the target was in the bar, the strike team would set out. A.J. would be the inside man and the shooter. She would be wearing club wear with the suppressed AMT Auto Mag .22 Magnum in a special holster Velcroed to the inside of her leg near her, well, high up on her leg. Once she had ID'd the target, dialing a preset on her cell would result in her cover team going into action. When Manuel had first handed the weapon to her, A.J. had dropped the magazine and cleared the weapon. She held it up and looked down the barrel.

"Manuel, there's a problem. The suppressor hides the front sight. How can you aim this thing?"

Manuel laughed. "It's true about almost any pistol. Once you screw a suppressor on it, it becomes a point-and-shoot weapon. Funny, they don't ever show that in the movies, do they?"

Anna was nervous but ready when she walked into the club. Out side there were two vehicles—a cheap Ford with a quarter kilo of C-4 under the gas tank and a taxi. Four men were outside, all with access to heavy automatic weapons as well as a radio detonator for the C-4. The amount of explosive had been carefully chosen. It should be enough to blow the car, possibly break some glass, and hopefully start a fire. The intent was to create a hell of a distraction outside the lounge, but not to cause any collateral damage.

The execution seemed easy. Once the explosives detonated, A.J. would pull out the suppressed .22, walk up behind the target, put two behind his ear, and walk away.

This op went exactly as planned. A.J. was in the lounge and had located the target. She checked his identity several times from several angles and even was able to verify the tattoo. She sent the cell message and placed her left hand close to the weapon. She had a different look tonight. No wig, her hair was short and had a nearly black rinse in it courtesy of Maria. From Maria's closet she had borrowed a pinstripe suit jacket and mini-skirt. She had joked with Maria, "This looks like it cams from Frederick's of Hollywood!"

"How did you know?" Maria had answered.

To complete the ensemble, A.J. had found some fishnet stockings and stilettos. She was hoping the outfit would keep anyone from frisking her at the door, and she turned out to be correct. She had deliberately worn rather outlandish, nearly Goth makeup.

When the car bomb out front detonated, the crowd went wild. The lounge was a semi-private club, unless you were a woman with a really short dress. When the C-4 outside went off, the shockwave and noise inside the lounge created instant panic. The power died, killing the lights, and creating excitement among Rico's bodyguards. The battery-powered emergency lights came on, creating a ghostly atmosphere in the lounge. The drop ceiling had erupted in dust everywhere, creating a foggy aura to the entire lounge. A.J. maneuvered to within a couple meters of the target. She had the High Standard in her left hand as she eased in closer. A bodyguard was in the way, so she grabbed his shoulder and slapped him in the face, loudly accusing him of grabbing her ass and questioning his parentage.

The bodyguard was holding a large caliber pistol in one hand as he shoved her with the other, calling her a crazy bitch. Rico turned to see what the commotion was but continued easing toward the door. A.J. saw the opening and brought the pistol up, pulling back the slide to chamber a round, then she changed to holding the gun in her right hand. Safety off, gun up, *pop pop*, two right behind the ear. She immediately dropped to her knees, depositing a Queen of Hearts card to the floor right under a collapsing Rico. A bodyguard to the target's right noticed his boss crumbling. All hell broke loose while A.J. crawled away from the throng of people massing around Rico. Once she got to the wall, she stood again, joining the mad press of people trying to get out the door to the street.

Several nervous minutes later, she cleared the door with the exiting crowd. A hulk of a car was burning twenty meters away to the left; consequently, everyone in the crowd was headed to the right. A.J. proceeded with the crowd. Twenty more meters allowed the crowd to thin out, and per plan, she turned right and walked down an alley to the back of the bar. She immediately recognized the cab and driver, so she simply hopped in the back and shut the door.

The cab delivered her to Manuel's house, and after nodding to the guards; she quietly slipped in and went to bed.

Morning found her with Manuel in his library. "Excellent job, Anna," Manuel said softly. "Word on the street this morning is Carlos is very upset. We think there's a possibility he's dropping out of sight, at least temporarily. That's the good news. The bad news is he has a 100k bounty on your head. Literally. He wants your head."

"That's good news, no? Doesn't it mean the hits and the playing cards are having the desired effect?"

"Yes, it does. But Tom and I have concerns for you. We're considering relocating you. Besides, if your playing cards start showing up on corpses hundreds of kilometers away, you'll be a legend. The fear factor will multiply exponentially. So, unless you have a problem, you're headed for Cali."

"Is that a good idea? I know people in Cali. It'll make it harder to keep my whereabouts secret."

"Don't worry, you won't be in Cali per se; we have an idea for a new cover to match your mission. Here's the thought; we don't know exactly where or when, but there's word of a something pretty big coming up. Tom wants to move you to a cover site we have near Cali. It's an oil exploration camp. It's twenty clicks outside the city. It belongs to Global Petroleum. Some of the people are really hunting oil, but we have about six guys there. They're all independent contractors, pretty much like you. Some are ex-SEALs, some Rangers, but all are contract employees."

"What am I going to do?"

"You're going to be a new engineer. Don't worry; everyone in the camp will keep their mouths shut. They're paid a lot to do so. It gives us a great reason to go in and out with helos as well as driving around in Land Cruisers."

"The cowboys don't object?"

"No, we pay off the local officials, spread around appropriate amounts of money."

"So, ultimately what will we be doing?"

"Ultimately, we'll want you and the team to help ruin their party whenever the deal goes down. We've got max intel resources on this. Tom says he's bringing in some whiz kid from No Such Agency. We'll have satellite priorities, the whole nine yards. It's a maximum effort, and you, Anna, are going to be squarely in the middle of it."

A.J. had a pretty good idea who the whiz kid was. She was missing her brother; she hoped she was right. Manuel asked A.J. to pack. She would be leaving that afternoon.

Sure enough, by 1300, a cab with two bodyguards arrived at the house. Manuel and Maria both hugged and kissed A.J., telling her they would see her soon and to take care. The cab headed for a small airfield ten kilometers out of town. The bodyguards stood by her as she collected her duffel bag. Soon she heard the distinctive *whup whup* of Huey blades approaching. A white helo landed on the tarmac. The side of the chopper displayed a "Global Petroleum" logo. She approached the chopper with her head slightly down even though she knew there was plenty of clearance between her head and the rotating blades. The bodyguards carried her bags as she approached the helo. The door opened, and a hand reached out to help her onboard. She sat down and looked across to the opposite facing seat; she was staring at a familiar face.

"Hi. How goes it, sis?"

"Never better, brother."

T.D. smiled as he closed the door, and A.J. grinned back at him as the bird lifted off, heading west.

Chapter 18

Global Petroleum Oil Exploration Site

30 Kilometers South of Cali, Colombia

Some five hours and two fuel stops later, the Global Petroleum helo landed at the compound near Cali. T.D. and A.J. made attempts to talk, but the high noise level in the Huey's cabin made it difficult. They did get to talk some during a fuel stop. The aircraft commander had told them they would be on the ground long enough for coffee and a bathroom stop.

A.J. looked at her brother. The young man sitting across from her looked the brother she remembered, brown hair, average height and build. A slightly shorter version of her Dad. T.D. didn't look like a hippy, but he certainly didn't resemble a stockbroker either. He was in jeans, sneakers, and a plain white tee with a photographers vest. He took off his Ray Ban aviator sunglasses and smiled at A.J. Those eyes seemed to look into her brain.

"So, little sister, heard you broke bad, started kicking some asses that really needed it, huh? What am I going to do with you?"

"T.D., if you were here, you'd have given me the green light all the way. I believe it with all my heart. So, you being here, does that mean the guys in suits at NSA decided they could loan you to us? How much have you been told? Oh shit, now I really feel like a turd. That's not the first thing I should be asking you. How are you? How are Mother… er, Mom and Dad?"

"It's okay, Alex, I know it's how your brain is wired, strictly business. Mom and Dad are fine. They were worried about you when they found out about the legal problems you had. I talked to Hendrix; he said you were right not to tell them until it was over. Mom and Dad would have gone ballistic. Sounds like you had some excitement, and from what I've heard, you're a force to be concerned about if you're on the wrong side."

"You haven't answered me, T.D. How are you?"

"I'm good. This gig with NSA is close to heaven for me. By the way, you look different. Harder, there's a look in your eyes, and yet you're prettier. Hot even. It looks good on you."

A.J. almost blushed. "So, how are you going to help us with the cowboys?"

"I have some equipment coming in tomorrow. I can tell you more then. We need to go. The pilots are waving to load up."

The sun was about to disappear over the horizon when the chopper landed in the compound. It looked like a bunch of single and doublewide trailers inside a double fence. When they exited from the helo, a tall, dark-haired guy that had ex-military written all over him met them. His clothes were khaki and his boots looked like military surplus jungle boots; in short, all he was missing were the bars or stripes of rank.

He held his hand out to T.D. first. "Mr. Moring I presume? And Miss DeJesus?" He shook A.J.'s hand as well. "I'm Kevin Strong. I run the camp for Global. Would you two please follow me?" He led them to a singlewide trailer and entered some numbers on the keypad lock. A small green light came on, and he opened the door and gestured them ahead of him. The two walked into an office that actually looked like an oil exploration office. There were maps, aerials, and what looked like seismic charts all over the wall. There were small differences too. The steel file cabinets that could be found in any office all had combination locks. There were two phones on Kevin's desk. One looked like a secure phone with an encryption box under it.

"Welcome to our humble home, folks. We have rooms for both of you; someone will escort you there in a few. First things first, Mr. Moring, I understand you have a trailer being helo'd in tomorrow morning. How big is it and what are your power requirements?"

"The trailer's eight by sixteen. It's set up for a hundred-amp service, but I can get by with sixty. I have power purifiers and battery backups, so if your generators are a little flaky, I'm still good."

"Smart, someone thought ahead for a change. What's in it?"

"Classified, Mr. Strong."

Kevin grinned. "Thought so, didn't hurt to ask though. Miss DeJesus, you're going to be a big part of our strike team I hear. Also hear you have an AKA. Queen of Spades? What's up with that?"

“Can I ask a few questions first, Mr. Strong?”

“Sure, fire away, pun intended.”

T.D. laughed; A.J. didn’t. “Mr. Strong, my current passport says Anna DeJesus on it. Obviously that’s not my name, but for now, can we stick with Anna?”

“Sure, but I’m fascinated. What’s up with the Queen of Spades shit?”

“It was my operational commander’s idea. Every time I make a kill, I leave a playing card, a queen of spades. I think it’s a head game, but he likes it.”

T.D. broke in. “It’s more than that. As you guys probably know, I’m NSA. We scoop up phone calls, landline, cell, doesn’t matter. Our computers listen for key words. They use them to filter out communications we might be interested in from all the other crap we don’t care about. That’s what I’ll be doing in the trailer, day and night. The agency has dedicated a lot of resources to this. We’ll have access to satellites, aircraft, illegal phone taps, you name it.”

“Is your trailer hardened, Mr. Moring?”

“Hardened? How?”

“These trailers we’re in. They may look wimpy, but they all have Kevlar in the floors, walls, and roofs. The few windows you’ll see are bulletproof and can’t be opened.

“No, I didn’t design for that,” T.D. admitted.

Kevin continued, “Our fences look pretty normal, but we have surveillance equipment out in the woods. We’ve got claymores. We’re loaded for bear as long as the bad guys don’t send an army.” He turned to A.J. “By the way, Anna, looking at what you brought in for equipment, I’m assuming you didn’t bring anything in the way of firearms other than maybe pistols. We have an armory you can check out in the morning. I'm assuming you brought your calling cards?"

A.J. nodded.

Kevin picked up a walkie-talkie, "Scooter, come to my office please." Scooter clicked his mike twice, and shortly there was a knock on the door.

"Come." A short young man entered. He didn't have a military appearance about him. "Scooter, please take our newest employees to their quarters and show them where the mess hall is. I'll join all of you for dinner in a few."

Scooter took the two new arrivals to a doublewide. He entered digits on a keypad and asked them to follow him in. They entered a large communal room with several couches and a TV. There were desks, some with computer terminals, and a couple bookshelves, one with VCR movies, the other with paperbacks. "Come on down the hall, you two." He stopped at one open door. "Take your pick, they're all the same. There's two baths with showers at the end of the hall, and there's a half bath off the rec room. Sorry, ma'am, but there's no separate facilities. Share and share alike so to speak. The locks do work, and you're not the only woman here."

"Take your pick ma'am. I'm probably going to spend most of my time in the trailer, so it really doesn't matter."

"Okay," A.J. replied, "I'll just take this one. Scooter, can we just drop our junk and go to mess? I am seriously hungry!"

T.D. laughed and nodded in agreement, and the two dropped their stuff. Scooter handed each of them a key card. It apparently operated the room door lock and was on a long chain. On the back there was a sticker with four digits. A.J. was turning the card back and forth en she looked up at Scooter.

"Wondering about the sticker?"

"Yeah, does it work the keypads?"

"Yep, but there's a slight wrinkle; the way the boss has it set up, everyone has a discrete number. We can tell who accessed what locks and when. Plus, your code will only open locks you have a reason to access; for instance, nobody can access the boss's trailer but him."

"I get it."

"Let's go to the mess hall, think it's Italian night."

The three stepped into the centrally located doublewide. They were in a large, open space that spanned almost the entire interior of the trailer. At one end there was what appeared to be a full bar with stools and everything. There was no bartender at the time; it appeared closed. In the middle segment, there were couches and chairs, and at the other end, there were six long tables with folding chairs. It resembled a cross between a military mess hall and the meeting area of a construction trailer. There was a small buffet area with steam warming racks.

Scooter had been correct. Lasagna was in the buffet, along with salad, rolls, and a cobbler of some sort. A fast-food style dispenser held soft drinks and tea. The three went through the line and took seats at an empty table. The other camp employees were scattered in groups at the other tables. It looked like a wide assortment of characters; long hair, crew cuts, and three other women. A.J. was willing to bet they were real oil workers. Two had ponytails and glasses and had "geek" written all over them. The third looked like she could bench-press a couple hundred pounds. She had short hair and was involved in a loud conversation with some other construction types.

Scooter, A.J., and her brother were half finished with their meal when Kevin showed up. "How's your dinner?"

he asked. He sat down with them, a tray in hand. He began to eat and talk.

“Great,” A.J. and T.D. answered simultaneously.

“Excellent. Anna, I had some uniforms dropped off in your room. Do you need any, Mr. Moring?”

“No, I’m good, and please, call me T.D. or Thomas.”

“Good enough, Thomas. I suppose you’ll be busy tomorrow getting your gear set up.” Kevin turned to A.J. “Miss DeJesus, I just got off the sat phone after a long conversation with Tom. He gave me a great deal of background on you. Tomorrow, while Thomas here is setting up his gear, you and I and our contract team will have a great deal of work to do getting acquainted. There’s also an op coming very soon. We’ll all discuss it together. If you’re finished with your dinner, why don’t we head for the bar? I’m about to open it.”

“Are you the bartender, Mr. Strong?”

“Yeah, guess you could say that. Bartender, owner, and bouncer as well. The bar was my idea. I open it whenever I feel it’s appropriate, and I close it when I think it’s time.” He stood, turned to the rest of the room, and announced, “Your attention please. Will the contract operators please join me at the bar? Some introductions are in order.”

Kevin walked to the bar with A.J. and her brother, motioned for them to pull up a stool, and walked behind the bar. He reached up and pulled a lanyard, ringing a bell. “The bar is officially open.” He placed a shot glass in front of all eight gathered at the front of the bar and commenced pouring out of a large bottle of Crown. “Let me introduce our newcomers. This young man is Thomas, or T.D. He’s on loan from NSA, and he’s going to be running our own private intelligence gathering system. The young lady here prefers to go by Anna for now. She’s a new contract operator, and she'll be sitting in on our morning brief. Before any of you make any assumptions, this is the lady who took on the cowboys that recently tried to off the DEA and Marine unit south of Cali."

A tall man with a blond crew cut walked up to A.J. and extended his hand. "I'm Pete, welcome aboard. That was you? I mean you were the one that saved your unit from the ambush? I'm impressed; you're a freakin' legend!"

A.J. shook his hand firmly. "If people are saying I saved us, it's bullshit. If the Air Force hadn't gotten there with an extraction team when they did, we'd have been heads on a stick. No doubt in my mind."

Another operator walked up. He, too, extended his hand. "Name's Cal. I'm from L.A., so I wound up as Cal. Anna, you might be right about the Air Force, but the report we saw said you carried a running gun battle single-handed for miles. Said you either shot 'em in the knee or the head. What was up with that?"

A.J. pushed her empty shot glass back toward Kevin with a look that said, "Refill please," and replied to Cal. "I'd always heard if you kill one, the others walk over him and keep coming. If you shoot him in the knee, he can't keep coming, and it takes two to carry him. Plus he's squalling like a baby. I didn't have a lot of ammo, so I shot them in the knees."

"But you shot some in the head."

"Well, some of them didn't take the hint."

At that point, the introductions were done, and the meeting graduated to shop talk.

"What were you shooting? M40-A1?"

"What range?"

"How much drop did you allow?"

A.J. was in her element. T.D. sat back and smiled. His sister had grown up, and she was a cold, calculating killing machine. Could he control her? Could anyone? It would be interesting. That much was for sure.

Chapter 19

Global Petroleum Oil Exploration Site
30 Kilometers South of Cali, Colombia

The meeting convened at 0700 in Kevin's trailer. The six, now seven, contract operators were there, T.D., and Kevin. That was it. Nobody had a hangover since Kevin had closed the bar after a little over an hour and several bottles of Crown.

"Anna, T.D., this op was in the planning stages before you two got here. We have intelligence indicating there will be a medium shipment of product leaving the area in the next week or so. Normally, a shipment of this size wouldn't be worth our involvement. We'd simply pass the intel Stateside and hope our guys back there would intercept the plane. This is apparently a new client, and the buy is being made in cash, at the point of transfer,"

Pete whistled. "Cool, how much, boss?"

"1.25 mill, U.S.," replied Kevin.

"Outstanding!" Pete exclaimed. He and the other operators started exchanging high-fives. A.J. looked at her brother; his face registered the same puzzled look she felt.

"From the look on your face, I'm assuming you're not aware of the bonus pool."

She shook her head.

"Tom set it up. Any cash deal we take down, this unit takes a 15 percent cut. Ten percent goes to the contract operators, split equally. Five percent goes to the camp. I take some, and the rest pays for booze, bribes to locals, payments to informants, sort of a miscellaneous slush fund. Tom didn't tell you when you went on contract status there'd be bonuses?"

"Well, he did say I'd get a substantial raise, and there were bonuses, but he was never specific."

Pete lightly patted her on the shoulder. "You could be a rich bitch when you leave here. Tom deposits our salaries and bonuses in offshore accounts. Didn't he set one up for you?" She nodded. "Well, assuming we leave here alive, we won't be needing gainful employment anytime soon."

"The exchange will take place here." Kevin pointed to a dirt strip that appeared to be about fifty clicks away. It was crowded in his small office. Kevin stood before a two by three meter map of the surrounding area. "We'll insert you guys early so you can scout the area and plan the takedown. The procedures we've used before involved taking down the guards. Once the plane and the money arrived, we've taken control of the situation. We take the money then call in a DEA team that helo's in and places all the participants under arrest. The plane and the dope are confiscated. At this point I leave this meeting. I don't want anyone knowing the actual operational details except you guys. Anyone have any questions?"

A.J. cleared her throat. "Yeah, being the newbie here, I have a couple. I don't see the Colombians surrendering with a smile. Maybe the pilots, but cowboys? I don't think so. Does anybody here actually think somebody won't pull a trigger?"

Pete looked at her and sighed. "They probably will. I can almost guarantee a shootout. That's why it's critical we work out where we'll be located so we can take them down."

"Then forgive me if I don't get it. What this sounds like to me is an ambush and theft of 1.25 million dollars. Felony murder, pure and simple. Am I wrong?"

Kevin looked at her. "You and I will discuss that later. You said you had a few questions? What were the others?"

"Well, I've already been through one op where DEA had bullshit intel and sent us into an ambush. How much confidence do we have in the intelligence? Do we know we aren't being lured into a trap?"

"That's a totally legitimate question. How about this; Mr. Moring here is new in country. He has no preconceived attitudes about it. I'll give him everything I have, he can review it, and we'll meet again to discuss it. By the way, T.D., the helo carrying your package should be here in about an hour. Please get with Scooter and get ready for your trailer. I assume we'll have to keep everybody out of the area; there'll be a lot of rotor wash. You two get busy." He turned to the contract operators. "You guys be discussing how you think we ought to handle the op." Turning to A.J., he said, "Why don't we take a walk? Maybe I can convince you we still have the moral high ground here."

The two walked out the door and headed toward the gate where the red clay road entered the camp. A.J. was dressed in fatigues and combat boots; as was Kevin. She could sense mutual respect even though they had just met. They walked through the gate and headed down the road.

"I can see why you would have reservations, but do you think these guys are all Boy Scouts? If this were a pure law enforcement operation, how would it be different? You'd yell, 'You're under arrest,' and then it's up to the bad guys. If they draw on you, you put them down."

"I get that part. This just feels different. It seems like we care about the money first, and anything else is secondary. I feel like a pirate, no, a privateer. Isn't that what they called them? Some king somewhere basically would give you a license to commit piracy on the high seas as long as the ship is flying the flag of your political opponent. Isn't that what we're doing?"

"Absolutely! It's the whole point, and it's what you're missing. It is all about the money; our objective is keeping the money out of the hands of the cartels. They're so sophisticated now they do their larger deals by freaking wire transfers; hell, they own the damned banks! When a cash deal comes along, we're going to take it down, and if we skim off the top to finance our operations so the U.S. Congress doesn't get wind of it, so be it."

A.J. was beginning to feel differently. She had been accused of seeing things in black and white. Maybe gray was acceptable sometimes. "Okay, I think I'm convinced. As long as these guys are armed, and as long as they have an opportunity to surrender, I'm in. By the way, it's been months since I've been able to run and do P.T. Is there a place here we can run without getting shot at?"

"Yeah, get with your team members. They'll let you run with them, I'm sure. I'm glad you feel better about the other. We're at war, remember that. The same people you're concerned about tried to kill you not that long ago. Keep that in mind!"

She nodded and shook Kevin's hand. About that time, she heard a low vibration off to the north. As the noise got closer, it became obvious they were hearing the twin rotors of a CH47 Chinook heavy-lift helicopter coming in with an olive drab rectangular box hanging under it. "Looks like my brother's toy box has arrived," she said.

"Yep, I'm not sure what he does, and I don't even want to know how, but it should be a huge asset to our operations."

"T.D. is very unusual, Kevin. He's an honest-to-God genius, but he has walking around sense too. It's a very unusual combination. I'm like you. I don't know what he does or how, but he's impressed some people I have a lot of respect for."

"I could say the same thing about you."

A.J. looked Kevin in the eyes. He was all business, but right now, he was flirting too. Hmm, he wasn't bad looking. He looked about thirty, but he was one of those guys that was difficult to judge. Tall, at least six-one, silvery, sandy crew cut hair, and the greenest eyes A.J could remember seeing on a man. He usually wore a semi-scowl on his face, but when he smiled a light came on. He had an infectious sense of humor when he chose to display it. If she didn't work with him… Oh well, something to consider.

The entire camp watched from a distance as the Chinook lowered T.D.'s trailer to the ground with guidance from Scooter and T.D. The helo wasn't on site more than five minutes; then it pivoted 180 degrees, the nose lowered slightly, and the chopper headed away to the north. Scooter had a crew scurrying under and around the trailer, tying it down to anchors while a second group began hooking up power.

A.J. had been standing fifty meters away, watching it all unfold. T.D. finally saw her and walked over. T.D. "I think I can be up and running in a couple hours. Right now, I'm going to start reviewing Kevin's intel about the exchange. I'll get back with your group by tonight sometime. Oh, by the way, Pete is looking for you. Something about you picking out some guns?"

It didn't take too long to locate Pete. He was in a conversation with one of the other contractors when A.J. walked up behind him and tapped him on the shoulder. "Pete, heard you were looking for me?"

"Yep. Come with me. We need to get you armed." He took off toward the mess hall. Instead of going in the front door, he walked to the back and keyed in his combination. "Come on in." He beckoned, allowing her to go up the concrete mobile home steps first. Once inside, he flipped on the lights.

"Holy shit, you guys have more stuff than we did in our Marine unit." She looked around the room. There was a rack of M16s, several grenade launchers, Soviet block RPZs, and even some belt-fed light machine guns.

"Grab an M16. Everybody has one of those. I've been thinking about the op. I want you to check this one out; we had a contractor Stateside build it just for us. I need you to get familiar with it." Pete opened a fiberglass case; inside was what looked like a modified M16, a very modified one. The stock was different; it had been adapted to allow a better sight picture through the Starlight scope. That scope would allow use in almost total darkness since it electronically magnified any natural light to show a nearly daylight view in a greenish hue. She had used one in training with the corps. The stock, scope and weapon itself were Parkerized in a matte black finish. There was a large suppressor on the end of the barrel. A daylight scope was in the case too.

"You'll need to practice with this thing. The balance isn't great, and the range isn't as good as a standard sniper rifle, but it will let you take down a target at night without telling anyone you're there. There's still just a little flash from the end of the suppressor, but it's only visible from the front. I think you should still be pretty effective out to about 300 meters. You have side arms from what I'm told?"

A.J. nodded. "I've got a suppressed nine and a suppressed .22 Mag. I don't think I'll need a handgun unless you feel differently."

"Okay, grab an M16. I'll carry the sniper rifle, and we'll take them to your quarters. You'll need to keep your door locked anytime you're not in there. I had Scooter add your key number to this lock, so if you need ammo, come and pick it up."

"Thanks, I'll practice tonight. By the way, when do you guys run? I've been working in the city, and I haven't run in forever. I don't want to get out of shape."

"Meet us at the mess hall at 0600. We'll have coffee, and then we'll run. The new NSA kid is supposed to give us some idea of what he's found out tonight. Think he's busy right now playing with his new toys."

They dropped the guns in A.J.'s room and then headed to the new addition to the camp. It already had a nickname. Above the door, someone had attached a hand-stenciled sign designating it as “The Black Hole.” Pete knocked, and T.D. came to the door after a few moments wearing headphones. “I’d ask you guys in, but then…”

“I know, you’d have to kill us,” A.J. said, completing the sentence for him. “How’s it coming?”

“Good, I’ve already got my computers talking to Fort. Meade, and they’re dumping feeds to me. We’ve got some planes and satellite sources gathering information as we speak. I’ve also requested some satellite shots of the potential landing site. I should have some daylight as well as infrared nighttime shots as long as the weather holds. They’re not going to reposition a bird for me, but if we have a few days, we’ll get something. That way we don’t have to go snooping ourselves and tip anyone off. I’ll let Kevin know when I can do a brief. Gotta get back to work…” He disappeared back into his little world, locking the door behind him.

A.J. and Pete looked at each other, kind of shook their heads, and walked away. Pete headed for the mess haul, and A.J. headed for her quarters.

The brief that night was after dinner. T.D. never came to the mess; he was in the Black Hole until the 1900 brief in Kevin’s office trailer. He walked in with his arms full of files, looking like he needed a shower, but still smiling like he knew a secret no one else did.

“Okay, here’s what I believe, guys. I’ve been able to correlate chatter both in Colombia and Arkansas about this deal, so I don’t think it’s a trap to lure us in. I can also tell you that there’s going to be pretty heavy security around the transfer. There appears to be some suspicion that a rival cartel is interested in getting either the dope or the cash, or both. The suspicion *could* be correct; I’m still working on that. Last, I have some very recent photos of the landing site. I've also made arrangements for an aircraft to do a flyover at very high altitude several hours before the deal goes down to see where the security teams are placed. You guys will already be in place, so I'll have to send word with coordinates or something. Anybody got any questions?"

Kevin looked over the photos and handed them to Pete. "T.D., any intel on when it's going to go down?"

"No, that seems to be top secret, probably more so than normal because of the fear of Carlos's cartel showing up."

"Carlos the Scorpion?" A.J. asked.

"Yes," T.D. replied with a somewhat subdued voice. A.J. wondered if T.D. or the guys knew she had a price on her head.

Kevin closed the meeting. "Pete, you need to get with your team and decide how you want to do this. I need to know what you need for support, but other than that, I propose you guys make the call of how you want to pull this off."

"Yessir," Pete replied.

"One more thing, remember, if you get the feeling that something's wrong, you guys have the option to abort. We're not defending anybody. If you don't like it, walk away, clear?"

Pete nodded, as did the rest of the contractors. They left the trailer in silence, each of them silently considering what the operation would entail. "Let's meet in the mess hall, guys. I'll lock the door; we can study the photos and go through some scenarios. We'll meet in thirty minutes."

At midnight, A.J. was about to go to bed. She was sitting on her bed in shorts and a tee shirt cleaning her M16. The meeting had lasted until 2300 hours, and she was too wound up to go straight to sleep, so she had decided it was a good time to clean a weapon. She hadn't been able to try out the sniper rifle, but maybe in four hours or so, she'd have a chance. There was a knock on the door. She recognized it. She had heard that knock for many years; it was T.D. She let him in.

"You aren't sleepy, sis?"

"No. What about you? And you need a shower; you stink."

"Okay, I'll go in a minute. I just wanted to see you a sec."

"What's up?"

"Well, I guess I'm just a little concerned."

"How so?" A.J. could see T.D. had something important in his eyes.

"Well, I know we agreed you were going to do this, the killing part and everything, but dammit, you're still my little sister. It's a little disconcerting to find out you're AKA the Queen of Spades and you have a bounty on your head. I just want you to be careful. Okay?"

She surprised herself a little with her next action. She stood and hugged him. Then she kissed him on the cheek. "I will, brother, I'll be careful. I promise."

"Okay, get some sleep, queen."

"I will. Get a shower!"

He nodded and left the room.

Chapter 20

Global Petroleum Camp

Cali, Colombia

A.J. was just beginning to feel the burn; she and her fellow contract operators were about seven or eight clicks out of the camp on their run. The sun was high enough above the horizon now to see around pretty well; it had been nearly pitch dark when they had left the camp.

Her feet hurt. It sounded crazy, as much as she had bitched to Isobel about the high heels, but breaking in new combat boots wasn't easy either. She had enjoyed the coffee, the camaraderie of a group that would trust one another with their lives. The contract operators had an entirely different mindset from the DEA people; not that the DEA people were somehow inferior, but the attitude was different. She felt much more accepted, less like an outsider with this group.

The run was helping her mentally too. Somehow it allowed her to focus more clearly on the ideas running through her brain, and one in particular was bubbling to the top. The prime objective in asymmetrical warfare was concentration of forces. The enemy could have more men, but the attacking force, in this case the men she was running with, could still be successful if they could overwhelm the enemy in a small, specific location. Standard doctrine was that a three-to-one numerical advantage was desired. They didn't have that, not even close.

She understood the objective was the cash. She felt there was a flaw in the existing plan of trying to take an area as large as the airfield with seven operators. It wasn't going to fly. They needed to allow the transfer and then follow the money, intercepting it in some location where they could totally overwhelm the cowboys charged with guarding and transporting the cash. She had decided to bounce this off T.D. first and then approach Pete in a one-on-one situation.

The group was on the way back to camp now, thank God. Not being able to run for a long period was telling on her. She was hurting everywhere! She had been noticing for a while now that she had migrated to the front of the pack. Pete was a meter to her left.

"Hey, Pete," she huffed.

"Anna."

"Why did the others fall back behind me?"

"Obviously you've never had the opportunity to see your ass while you're running."

"Oh." She had not. On the other hand, she could understand. She had never had too much trouble with guys talking to her chest. She knew they were appropriate for her build, but not that large. She had, however, had a fair number of compliments about her ass. She would have to thank her mother sometime; she was pretty confident that was where it had come from.

"Pete, can we talk after we get back?"

"Sure, something wrong?"

"No, wrong isn't the word I would use. I may have an idea. I want to run it by T.D. and then bounce it off you guys." Her wind was actually coming back, and either the boots were beginning to break in or she was becoming numb to the pain. She would survive after all.

T.D. actually had a lot on his plate. He was waiting on a satellite pass so he could upload a dump of data to Fort Meade and anticipated a download of transcribed telephone calls that might be of interest. On the other hand, it would be an hour, and his sister had given him "that look." She had always been able to get him to do almost anything with the look. He would have described it as a sad puppy look. *She's so proud. This must be really important to her to want my opinion.* Hence, he was walking out the gate with her.

"Okay, A.J., what's up?"

"Well, it's this op the guys want to do, taking down the drug deal and stealing the cash."

"What about it?" It hadn't sounded that complicated to T.D.

"Look, how many bad guys would you have there if you were bringing over a million cash? Twenty? More? There's seven of us. Granted, we'd have the element of surprise, but we'd be spread so thin due to the large area. It's a freakin' runway for Christ's sake. We could take four or five down with the sniper weapons before they get organized, but after that, game on."

"I get it. Plus, what we talked about is almost a certainty. The Scorpion dude is definitely going to try to take the cash and the coke. That means another wad of bad guys. You're right. You guys should probably take a pass on this one."

"You know that for a fact, brother? Carlos is coming?"

"Yes, well, his people. I can't verify he's going to be there in the flesh."

"Doesn't matter, that's not what I was thinking. I've got an idea; I'll run it by Pete. Thanks, T.D." She turned to walk back to her quarters.

"But…" T.D. shook his head. He hadn't actually discussed much of anything with her. He just walked with her while she thought. Normally, he would be frustrated, but knowing his sister, he understood. They *had* discussed it, just on a non-verbal level. Neither of them understood it. She could use the odd ability better than he could, but it was there. The two had realized it existed since they were pre-teens; was it E.S.P.? Just an ability to read facial expressions? He didn't know, and he doubted she did, but they both understood it existed. He could tell she had a plan; she could be devious. She had abilities that frightened him at times. His second sense didn't tell him what the plan was, but there was definitely something cooking in her mind.

"So, basically what you're trying to tell me, is my plan sucks, and you've got a lot better idea?" Pete was pissed as they walked around the camp. A.J. had anticipated some pushback. She didn't want to have a pissing match in front of the other contract operators. Her shower and some fresh clothes had solidified her plan.

"You make it sound worse than it is, but yeah, pretty much. T.D. is going to tell us Carlos is going to try to steal the money and the coke. There'll be thirty, forty cowboys there, maybe more. There's seven of us. I'm hardly a tactical genius, but those odds suck. Here's my plan. We back off and watch. There should be only one way in and out of the runway. We let Carlos's people come in, steal the money. Hopefully the two little armies will take each other down a tad in numbers. The winner will haul ass with the money and the coke. We do like Woodward and Bernstein said and follow the money. Then we steal it. They'll be hauling ass out of the runway area; we pick a spot, hit 'em with an RPG, and then hit the van with a lot better numerical odds." She had been watching Pete's face the whole time. His face had gone through a gradual transition, from pissed to inquisitive to nearly a smile.

"You're a deceptive little bitch, you've got a nice ass, and I like the way you think. You're right. We don't need to control the whole runway. We really just want the money. I like your plan. I want you to present it to the group at the brief tonight."

"No."

"No? Why not? It's your idea, and it's great. Why not?"

"Pete, you're the team leader. You have their trust, their respect. This group isn't like a normal squad. You guys are all Alpha dogs. I'm the new bitch in town, and nice ass or not, they're going to buy into an idea that came out of your mouth long before one that comes out of mine. No. It'll work a lot better if you present the plan. Just say because of Carlos's people being there, we're changing the plan. One more thing. I trust you guys. I'm sure you know my real name isn't Anna. When I was a Marine, I went by A.J., or LT. I'd like the guys in our team to call me that."

He nodded, "You're smart, A.J., and you have perception that doesn't normally come with someone your age. We'll do it your way, but we'll say it's mine. By the way, you're right about the guys, but you're wrong about yourself. I think we're dealing with an Alpha bitch." He smiled and slapped her back. "See you at the brief."

The final plan emerged after several planning sessions and mock attacks, using the road to and from the Global Petroleum camp as the substitute for the road into the clay airstrip. There were also several mock runs to a location near the strip to verify how long it would take to get there. A.J. got to test fire the sniper rifle several times, in daylight and darkness. They were assuming they would have no more than twelve hours notice. Using aerials supplied by T.D. from satellite, they had driven the Toyotas to within about ten kilometers of the airport. They didn't want to be seen near the property. They had set up survey equipment to make it look like oil-related work. What they'd actually been doing was planting microphones in the road. The devices had transmitters that would send to a central receiver in the woods. The receiver had a repeater with enough range to be picked up anywhere in the area. With all that done, and one last run-through, they were ready. Weapons were checked and re-checked. They were on ready alert now, waiting on intel from T.D.

There had been another minor surprise, at least to A.J. Scooter, the go-to guy in the camp, would be coming with them. He wasn't an operator, but he would coordinate all the communications. He would have an open line to T.D. back at the base and another to Pete. He would be listening to the microphones and would be staged to put eyes on the road about two clicks up the road from the field. They were ready.

A.J. mulled it back and forth in her mind. Was stealing money from criminals a crime? Did it really matter? An answer never came, and she eventually fell asleep on the couch in the lounge area of the doublewide her room was in.

Chapter 21

The Runway

1600 hours local time

A.J. was seated, more or less comfortably, about twenty feet up a tree. Cal was her cover, at the base of the tree watching her back. Her job was to watch the exchange, to follow the money. The majority of the other operators were several hundred meters off the access road. Their job would be to cut off the escape route of the money. As soon as the transfer was made, A.J. and Cal would be running to catch up with the rest of the team.

A.J. was comfortable to be back in camo again. She was wearing camo pants and shirt over another black halter. She and Cal both had their ballistic vests and were both wearing ball caps. A.J. was looking through binoculars at the runway. She heard Pete announce T.D. had sent word the probable drug plane was about five minutes outbound. T.D. obviously had someone telling him that, but of course, it was classified. Everyone in the team was wearing an earpiece and a small boom mike. The push-to-talk button was at her waist. The sniper rifle rested across her lap.

The group had watched from their various vantage points as three large vans had come down the road. Once they had entered the large cleared area runway sat in, one van had begun to offload cowboys carrying what looked like MAC 10s every few hundred meters. One or both of the two remaining vans had to be carrying the coke. The money should be on the plane.

About that time, someone in the group clustered midway down the runway popped some orange smoke; doubtless it would serve to confirm the correct field and to show the pilots the wind direction and a clue of the wind speed.

As she watched, A.J. heard Pete come up on the com in a quiet voice." All units, be advised T.D. is reporting lots of chatter on the cell numbers used by group two. Keep your heads down please and watch each other's backs. Acknowledge please."

A.J. waited her turn and replied, "Watcher copies." She continued to gaze with the binoculars off to the northeast until a small dot was visible just above the horizon. A fairly good-sized twin-engine cargo plane appeared. T.D. had briefed them that the plane had left Arkansas. For some reason A.J. was unaware of, Arkansas was a new center for drug importation into the U.S. She suspected as usual that money and politics were in play. The aircraft overflew the runway once to assess the conditions and began a turn to line up for an approach into the wind. Within a few minutes, the aircraft was taxiing up to the group clustered around the two vans.

Although she was about 250 meters away, A.J. could clearly see what was going on. The cabin door opened, and two men exited; one about forty, the other in his twenties.

"Aircraft down, engines stopped," A.J. quietly announced.

"Copy," Pete replied. "Be advised, we have incoming forces. We're hearing what sounds like heavy traffic on the road, and we suspect dirt bikes in the jungle. Everybody stay low!"

Pete, T.D., and A.J. had speculated how Carlos and his men would try to wrap up the large area involved. None had thought of the dirt bikes, but it was a logical and innovative approach. As A.J. watched the transaction in progress on the runway, it seemed apparent none of them were aware The Scorpion's men were only moments away. In the meantime, the money had appeared in two large black suitcases and was being counted. The coke, loaded in the back of one van, was being sampled in a manner remarkably similar to the methods shown on *Miami Vice* and in the movies.

"Asset is in two black suitcases. Will advise vehicle as soon as possible," A.J. announced to the net. Several single mike clicks indicated she had been copied. A few moments later, the scene began to unfold.

"All units, a heavy truck is coming down the road, looks like a fuel truck."

A.J. listened, thinking that part fit. The aircraft would need fuel prior to heading back to the States.

"Three or four pickups behind it. They've got machine guns mounted on two of them. Keep us filled in, Watcher. Looks like it's going down." Pete sounded excited.

"Copy," A.J. answered. She could hear the bikes coming as well, from several directions, the only part they hadn't anticipated. But as long as none of the riders spotted any of the operators, it might be okay. She watched through the binoculars as the fuel truck pulled up right by the vans and the plane. The Cartel Blanco crew didn't look surprised at the fuel truck's arrival, nor did the pilots. The cartel selling the dope had been prepared, but not for the onslaught of a small army, an army with a Trojan horse. The truck had appeared normal, maybe a 1500-gallon truck with a local logo. The truck also had side bins, bins that might normally hold hoses. In this case, they held half a dozen members of Carlos's group, all armed with submachine guns. At the same time those men unloaded and began firing, the pickups entered the clearing, guns blazing at the scattered guards up and down the runway.

Cartel Blanco returned fire, but it was over in less than a minute. The pilots had realized they were in the middle of a shitstorm and had stood with their arms above their heads.

"Shit's hitting the fan Pete. Group two has control of the scene. Stick with original plan, sir?" A single click was an answer in the affirmative. A.J.'s job was to delay any vehicles that might be escorting the cash as it left the field. She looked the situation over one more time with the binoculars to get a last look with a wide field of view. She picked up the rifle and got a good sight picture of the cash.

Carlos's men loaded the suitcases in one of the vans. Four men entered the van, two in front, two in the back, closing the back doors as they entered. Two more jumped in the second van, the one with the dope, and the vans did a one-eighty and started down the road. The driver of the fuel truck abandoned it and headed for one of the pickups. Before the pickup could move, A.J. sent a 5.56 round down the 250 meters aimed at the head of the driver. The next round went to the front tire. She quickly shifted to the truck with a machine gun closest to the road leaving the airport clearing. One round took down the man operating the gun; the second eliminated the driver. The rifle she was using had a thirty-round magazine. It was suppressed. She anticipated having a short time before anyone realized where the rounds were coming from. Then it would be time to scoot. Cal would let her know when it was time to go.

The two vans were headed down the road; the rest of the team would handle them. She shifted to the other pickup with the machine gun. It was moving, a radically more difficult shot. She shifted to pumping rounds into the cab. Apparently one finally found its target because the truck slewed to the left and stopped. As she watched, she saw the gunner in the back swing his Soviet block light machine gun right at her. The jig was up. She was looking dead into his eyes when he opened fire. It only took about a second or so, but it felt like slow motion. Her dad had told her about it, the strange expansion of time, almost like a slow-motion movie. She watched fire spit from the barrel of his gun. She felt her finger slowly pull the three pounds of pressure required to compress her trigger. Her crosshairs were between the cowboy's eyes. She never heard the weapon go off, but she did feel the slight recoil.

Just as she saw the cloud of red mist behind the man's head, her entire world exploded. Rounds hit the tree she was in; she literally felt the shock wave of supersonic lead missiles pass her head, and then her conscious thoughts came to a screeching halt when she was kicked in the sternum by an unbelievable impact.

So this is how it feels to die!

Cal heard a noise above him; he could hear the rounds impacting the tree. He looked up to see her rifle falling from the tree. Strangely, he was actually able to catch it. He looked up to see A.J. hanging from her safety line. Her eyes were partly hidden behind her yellow shooting glasses, but they looked closed. “A.J…A.J…, answer me, goddammit!”

Cal heard a noise; a dirt bike was hauling ass toward them. Cal kneeled by the tree and waited. There were three bikes coming at them, guns blazing. He slowly followed them as they approached. He took the first at about seventy meters, the second at fifty, and the third at twenty. *Thank God it’s hard to aim riding a motorcycle!* After each shot, he yelled up the tree again, “A.J…A.J…*A.J.,* answer me, dammit!”

Damn it hurts! How can it hurt so bad if you’re dead? And should people be yelling at me?

She was hurting and hearing; ergo, she wasn’t dead. As she cleared her fogged brain, she heard motorcycles, shooting, and Cal. He was yelling at her. He was cursing her, the fucker! “Cal! Don’t fucking cuss me, you ass!”

“A.J., get your ass down here. Time to go!”

She looked around; her safety line was holding her to the tree. She unhooked the carabiner as she sat up. Time to go! She started climbing down.

Shit, that hurts!

“I’m coming, dammit. Where’s my gun?” She looked down to see Cal had it. She dropped the last eight feet.

Shit! Everything hurts! Especially breathing.

Cal was holding her gun.

“A.J., can you run?”

"Cal, I'll try. I think I took a round to the chest. I guess the vest got it, but I'm hurting, man; I think I've broken some ribs."

She could see Cal looking around. She saw him staring at one of the dirt bikes. He ran to the bike, dragged the dead cowboy off, and fired it up. He pulled up to A.J. "Get on. Why run when we can ride? Probably still hurt like a bitch though. You're not coughing any blood, are you?"

"No, not that I can tell, go!" She climbed on the bike behind Cal. It wasn't a moment too soon. They had attracted attention. She could hear gunfire behind them as they made their way to the dirt road, and then Cal poured on the throttle. She heard him in her earpiece.

"Control, this is Spotter. We're coming at you on a trail bike, company behind us. Watcher's with me; she's been hit, copy?" A simple click came back. As the bike rounded a bend in the woods a kilometer down the road, the two could see smoke. The first van was on fire; the second had impacted a tree. The contract operators were snatching the suitcases out of the back and throwing them in the second van. Two operators were dragging bodies out of the second van.

A.J. was still weak when Cal skidded to a stop at the back of the second van; Pete and Scooter pulled her off the bike and threw her as gently as possible into the back of the van. One and a quarter million dollars worth of coke made a poor bed. Two other team members were moving to the rear of the van with M-79s. One started firing smoke grenades down the road; the other was pumping CS canisters in the same direction.

Pete reached into A.J.'s vest pocket and grabbed some playing cards. He scattered them on some of the bodies. The whole team piled into the van with Cal driving. He backed away from the tree, straightened out in the road, and headed out at a high rate of speed. The back doors were left open, and two of the operators were seated looking out the back, M-16s in hand.

"Let's take a look at you, A.J." Pete undid the Velcro of the vest and pulled out the ceramic plate. He looked her chest over beneath the vest. "No blood, A.J., that's a good sign. Still not tasting any blood or coughing up any, are you?" She shook her head. Pete undid her shirt and pulled up her halter. A.J. hadn't bothered with a bra; she didn't really need one with her relatively small boobs. She saw Pete's eyes grow wide and looked down as well as well as she could. There was a large red mark in her chest that was rapidly beginning to turn blue; it was going to be ugly in a day or two. As he ran his fingers along her ribs, she took a swing at him.

"Shit, Pete! That hurts, dammit!"

"Ribs, A.J. Looks like the rest is just a deep bruise. We'll need some x-rays. Take a rest while Scooter's doing his deal." He pulled some pills out of a packet in his vest, He motioned for her to open her moth and placed them on her tongue as he grabbed for a water bottle.

A.J. carefully craned her head around; Scooter had some sort of device he was running across the suitcases.

"They're bugged, boss. We gotta dump the money out to see if the bugs are in the suitcases or the cash." Scooter pulled some duffel bags out of his pack and began stuffing wrapped packs of hundreds into the bags. When four duffels were full, he ran the meter over the duffels and the suitcase again. "It was definitely the suitcases, Pete. The duffels don't register."

Pete nodded. “Stop the van, Cal!” They skidded to a stop. Steam was beginning to vent from under the hood. “C’mon, Scooter, grab a suitcase.”

Pete and Scooter each took a case, ran fifty meters out in the woods, and covered the suitcases with branches.

“Take off!” Pete yelled again climbing back in the van. “A.J., are you okay to walk?” She nodded. “Good, we’re coming up to the last part of the getaway. A couple clicks up the road, we’ll be leaving the van. We’re gonna have to walk about five clicks; are the pain pills kicking in yet?”

“Yeah, I’m feeling a little better. I think I can walk okay.”

“Good. As we discussed, we don’t want to have any of the cowboys thinking we’ve got their money and went back to the Global camp. T.D. has alerted DEA. They’ve got two choppers on the way. We dump the van and hike five clicks to another road. DEA should pick up the dope, their guys will keep the cowboys occupied, and about midnight, we’ll be picked up by Global trucks. By the way, the Queen of Spades is gonna be really unpopular. We left some of your cards near the airport, and of course, I dropped a few in the empty suitcases the cash was in.”

A.J. smiled. “Scorpion will go nuts!”

“Guaranteed! Just hope he doesn’t go over the top, or we’ll have to have you laying low.”

“The way I feel right now, I’m going to be laying low anyway.”

Pete nodded. “I think that would be best. I want the medic to look at you when we get back.”

The next twelve hours were a blur for A.J. She remembered walking. Every single step hurt, and having to breathe in little shallow gasps didn’t make it any easier. She remembered camping near the road and vaguely recalled being helped into the back of a truck. She woke briefly back at camp. The camp medic ran some x-rays and gave her a shot in her arm. Then her brain shut down, and sleep wrapped her in a warm cocoon.

Chapter 22

Global Petroleum Camp

A.J. was dreaming. She was in her bedroom in Fredericksburg; someone was calling her. It was her brother, T.D.

"A.J., time to get up. Alexandra Jane Moring, time to get up."

Now that was odd. T.D. never called her that. What the…

"A.J., you've been out for twelve hours. Time to get off your ass!"

Why, that prick! How dare he! She opened her eyes; it was fuzzy. She wasn't at home, but it was T.D. He was all grown up! He was wearing a tee shirt and jeans and sporting about a three-day beard. She tried to sit up. *Shit! What was that pain in her chest?* "Crap, T.D., why am I hurting, and where are we?"

“We’re at the Global Petroleum camp, A.J. You’re in your quarters, and twenty-four hours ago you took a round to the chest. Your vest pretty much stopped it, but we’d really like for you to get up and get a shower, maybe eat something, and let the medic take another look at you. Sound okay?”

She nodded and eased to an upright position. It was coming back now. They had pulled it off! She wanted details on the aftershocks of the op, but a shower did sound really good. T.D. tossed her a robe. She looked down; she was wearing a halter, panties, and nothing else. “Who put me to bed?”

“I got elected. We figured I’d seen it all before anyway. Once they gave you the shot, it was lights out, sis. How’s the chest?”

“Better. It hurts though. Glad they spent money on really good vests. It was a light machine gun round, not some wimpy 9 mm.”

“How did you know?”

“I saw him turn the gun on me and fire. Our rounds probably waved at each other as they passed. A vest wouldn’t have helped him.”

“Head shot?”

“Yep, and I know it was on the mark too.”

“Well, Kevin says it went real good. He wants to see you after the medic is through. Can’t have the Queen of Spades out of action, can we?”

She laughed. “No, guess not. Wait out in the big room. I’ll be out in a few.”

An hour later, after a long shower, breakfast, and a checkup with the medic, A.J. was seated in Kevin’s office with T.D. and Pete.

Kevin started off. “Well Anna, or A.J., from what I understand, the raid was a total success. Cartel Blanco lost their coke. Someone in Arkansas lost a pile of cash; and Carlos, who expected to get both, got nothing. By the way, from what we’re hearing, as well as what T.D. is saying, he’s quite upset. With you, A.J. Pete, comments?”

“Well, we’re all happy the op went well, and we are very proud of our new team member. Cal was in a position to see much better than the rest of us, but he says she’s a very cool cookie. Doesn’t rattle, shoots like a laser. Oh, and we’re very happy to have increased the bonus fund by a lot!”

“What’s the chatter this morning, T.D.?”

“Well, it’s very obvious to me the raid was a huge intelligence success. We’ve gained contacts to watch here in Colombia, as well as in Arkansas. There’s been so much traffic it’s added a heap to our pool of cell numbers and landline numbers. The landline numbers also yield a physical address. Another thing, we’ve got some new abilities coming on line, and the agency is using this operation as a test. We can now use computers to analyze speech patterns, almost like a fingerprint. So, with that ability, if someone like Carlos comes up on a new phone, after a period, we’ll be able to recognize him. Then we can monitor that number as well as the others.” T.D. looked around the room. Other than his sister, the others had zoned out.

“Okay, I’ll try again. The chatter is Carlos is about to have a stroke. He thinks A.J. and the DEA put it to him. He’s raised the bounty on you to a million, sis.”

Pete interrupted, “Wait, you guys are related?”

T.D. replied with a sheepish grin, “Yeah, ‘fraid so. Anyway, back to Carlos; he’s also planning on retaliating against the DEA. We're very concerned about that, but we hope he gets sloppy due to his anger. We would just like to avoid him blowing up another building and killing a lot of innocent people. When he did that in Cartagena, he pissed off a lot of locals, people who had looked up to him like a Robin Hood kinda guy. Anyway, he knows you're in Cali now, A.J."

Kevin looked at A.J. "How are you? We were all very concerned when we heard you were hit. Especially your brother; he was professional, but he was about to go nuts until he heard it looked like the vest saved you."

"I'm good. The medic says it's bad, but he's seen a lot worse. He says I'll be really sore for a week or two, and it should be completely gone in about a month."

Kevin smiled. "That's good news. I spoke to Tom this morning. He's delighted, but he's concerned as well. As of right now, our number one priority for T.D and our agents is to get a location on Carlos and then to terminate him. He was crazy before, and he's beyond crazy now. Tom would like you out of here, out of the country as a matter of fact. How long can we keep you, T.D.?"

"They aren't yelling too bad yet. It wouldn't be so bad, but they act like I'm on a vacation. Hell, I'm sleeping three hours at a time. But I can stay two, three weeks?"

"Great! Anna, A.J., soon as Tom figures out a safe place to stash you, you're outtahere. Take a week or so, and let Tom know how you are, okay?"

"I guess. Could I talk to Tom sometime today? I really don't want to go, but on the other hand, I guess I'm actually a hazard to the rest of you, and I'm not a lot of use right this minute anyway."

"I'm glad you see that," Kevin agreed. "You're right. I think Tom figures if he gets you out of country it lowers the risk for the rest of us getting blown up when they try to get to you. We'll get the word on the street you're going back to Cartagena. That ought to keep them confused for a bit. By the way, when you have a chance, get with Scooter. He can fill you in on your offshore account balance. It'll be going up. Anything else anybody?"

A.J. was carefully walking back to the mess trailer when her brother caught up. "I hope you realize how much you scared me, sister!"

"I'm sorry, believe me, it wasn't deliberate. The guy got off a lucky shot."

"Two hundred fifty meters with a machine gun? Doesn't sound lucky to me. Sounds like he just hosed out lead at the tree you were in. Cal said he could feel some of the rounds hitting the trunk. He said he never heard you return fire. He told me when he first looked up he knew you were dead. I knew when we discussed this way back when that there was a possibility of something bad happening to you. Can you imagine what our parents went through? Our Dad got wounded in the head, Mom was kidnapped once, my God, it must have been terrifying for them!"

"You're right, T.D., everything you said, but do you have any idea what a rush it is? I know I'm seriously screwed up in the head; I get it. I should be thinking this person in my scope has a wife, a girlfriend, parents. But since I don't, there's this rush. All my senses go into overdrive. Dad tried to describe it; I didn't get it at the time, but everything shifts into slow motion. It's exciting and terrifying all at the same time, kinda like the feeling normal people get at a horror movie amped up a hundred times…"

“I know. I think I understand. Just try to use what little empathy you’re capable of to appreciate how concerned I get, okay?”

“I will.” She kissed him on the cheek and walked in the mess hall. She had already had a light breakfast, but she was still hungry as a horse. The smell of burgers had been wafting through the compound as she walked. It was a temptation her stomach was telling her to yield to; and she was about to do just that.

“Hey, Tom, it’s A.J.” Kevin handed her his sat phone right after lunch and left his office to let her speak in private.

“A.J., good to be talking to you. We had a bit of a scare.”

“Yeah, sorry about that. I just couldn’t resist getting another round or two off. Note to self, shoot & scoot next time.”

“I guess Kevin told you I want to move you.”

“He did.”

“You need to be on the Global Petroleum helo this afternoon. It’s classified, but you’re going to Panama. There’s a CIA station inside Howard Air Force Base. I called in a few favors. I thought you needed a week or two to get back up to speed. I was debating where I was going to hide you and how much manpower it would take to properly guard you, and then I thought, hell, I’ll let the taxpayers pay for your security. So, you’ll be inside an Air Force base. I think they’re going to put you up in the bachelor officers’ quarters. You’ll have a pool and a bar!”

“What else could a girl ask for? Thanks.”

“One other thing. I’ll come to see you, but I still have concerns about having a leak inside our organization. I want to discuss it in private.”

"Do you think it's here in the Global camp?"

"Negative. I'm positive it isn't. I'll tell you how I can tell in person. Oh, one more thing. I told Kevin he could keep your brother a couple more weeks, and he probably can, but he will be moving soon as well. I've gotta go, A.J., be seeing you soon."

"Ten-four, see you soon." The loss of signal tone came up, telling her Tom had terminated the call on his end.

She returned left Kevin's phone on his desk and headed for T.D.'s Black Hole trailer. She knocked, and T.D. came to the door. "What's up?"

"I'm leaving this afternoon, on the Global helo shuttle. It's classified, but I'll be in Panama."

"Good. I'll miss you, but it'll be good to know you're safe."

She kissed T.D. on the cheek and returned to her quarters to pack. It didn't take long. Then she ran down Pete to tell him goodbye. He shook his head. "Are you coming back?"

"I don't know, Pete. I go where they send me, you know?"

"Yeah, I understand. You were a good fit. The guys respect you. Well, that's the way it is. We'll all miss you. Good luck wherever you wind up and good hunting." Pete hugged her.

Shit, that hurts!

"Thanks, Pete, now I've gotta go tell Kevin. You guys stay safe, okay? Keep all your Alpha dogs in check!" She shook his hand, and that hurt a lot less!

The conversation went along similar lines with Kevin. He acted disappointed, but understood. This time she reached out to shake his hand. When he spread his arms to hug her, she backed away. "Sorry, Kevin, Pete did that before I could think about it, and it hurt like a bitch. Nothing personal, but can we just shake?"

He laughed. "Sure, I get it." They shook hands, and then Kevin picked up his walkie-talkie. "Scooter, can you come to my trailer please?"

Scooter was there in a minute. "Yessir?"

"Scooter, when you hear the Global helo, please go to Miss Dejesus's quarters and carry her gear to the helo. Unfortunately she's leaving us today on the shuttle."

"Sorry to hear that, Anna. We'll miss you."

"Me too, Scooter. I think I'll be seeing you guys again. I'm still new at this, but I'm thinking this is a pretty small club. I hope to see all you guys again." They shook too.

About 1300 hours, the helo landed. A.J. walked out to it wearing fatigues and boots. She had thought briefly about it, and it seemed appropriate if she was going to be a guest on a U.S. military installation. Scooter carried her duffel bag out and put it in the bird once the incoming supplies were offloaded. The small Global ground crew proceeded to fuel the Huey while A.J. waited on the steps of the mess trailer. She hadn't noticed a small group gathering around the helicopter until she was summoned to board.

T.D. walked her out to the chopper and helped her board. He handed her a laptop in a case. It was only when she turned around that she noticed all the contract operators. Kevin and Scooter had snuck them into position at the side of the helicopter and were standing with T.D. When she waved, the entire group responded with a salute, a somewhat unorthodox one. They were saluting with their right hands and holding up a queen of spades with their left. Laughing, she returned the salute and took a seat. The crew chief slid the door closed and spun his right hand in a circle, signaling the pilots to spool up the turbine.

As the helo rose, the men on the ground waved once and then turned to return to their jobs. She had a chance to wave once before the pilot banked and turned to the north. For a brief moment, she was tempted to shed a tear, but the urge passed quickly, and she closed her eyes in an effort to nap.

Chapter 23

Howard Air Force Base

Balboa, Panama

A.J. felt a little silly. She was sitting on a lounger by the officers' club pool. She felt silly because rather than lying out in a bikini like the few other women there at the time, she was in a black halter top and camo shorts. The halter was because she had a rather stunning display of purple and green decorating her chest. She didn't want to gross anyone out. The shorts were because they were all she had; the two stunning bikinis she had bought in Mexico were probably still in the pile of debris that was formerly her apartment in Cartagena.

One lovely part of South and Central America were the piña coladas. She had not researched the details sufficiently to determine if it was the fresh coconut milk or the local rum. Whatever the cause, the effect was marvelous. Especially on top of a pain pill. She was glad Tom wasn't coming in until tonight; it would give her time to sober up, somewhat.

"Mind if I sit down?"

A.J. looked up to see a young lady standing next to her. The woman appeared to be in her late twenties; she was average height and build and looked like she was active duty based on her haircut. She was wearing a bikini, but it was a rather modest one. A.J. assumed there was probably a written or unwritten rule about appropriate attire at the officers' club.

"Sure, go ahead."

The girl sat on the lounger next to A.J. and offered her hand. "I'm Nancy, and I'm a captain with the meteorological unit. What's your story? Are you in the BOQ?"

A.J. had to think. What was she at liberty to say? Oddly, the subject had never come up. "Hi, Nancy, I'm Anna. Yes, I'm in the BOQ, and without trying to be rude, I really don't think I should say much about who I work for.

"That's okay. We get your types through here on occasion. They're usually guys though. Don't worry, I have no interest in going to prison. We've been told if we ever discuss anything about you transients we can wind up in Leavenworth. I'm not trying to be rude, but would you like me to loan you a bathing suit? We look like we're about the same size. I'm guessing you have to travel light."

"Maybe I'll take you up on that, depends on how long I'm here. I need for this to fade some." A.J. leaned forward a little and pulled out the scoop neck of her halter.

"Holy shit! Car wreck?"

A.J. thought again. What the hell. “No, actually it was a 7.62 machine gun bullet that my vest stopped. I’m supposed to be recuperating.”

“Wow, I’ve never met anyone who’s been shot. It must take balls to be somewhere with lead flying. Did they get him?”

“Who?”

“The guy that shot you.”

“They didn’t, but I did. You might say it’s my area of expertise.”

“Remind me not to piss you off, girlfriend!” Nancy was smiling, “Want another drink? I’m headed for the bar.”

“Please, and I think I’ll take you up on the swimsuit as long as it’s a one piece.”

“Yeah, I’ve got a one piece. Where are you eating tonight?”

“Probably here in the dining hall.”

“Okay, if I miss you tonight, I’ll leave it at the desk in a bag for Anna.”

“Thanks, Nancy, they want me to start swimming as soon as I can. They say it’ll speed my recovery up more than lying around.

Nancy returned with the drinks. They sat in their loungers and continued with girl talk. A.J. had never been really good at girl talk, but she had gradually acquired an ability to fake it fairly well. Nancy was mildly irritating, but not too bad. She seemed to be fascinated with trying to pluck stories of A.J.’s sexual escapades with her fellow spies. A.J. answered with the truth, which Nancy refused to accept. A.J. faked falling asleep, and thankfully it worked.

A.J. woke up on the chaise by the pool; Nancy had left. She grabbed her towel and requested a car for a ride back to the BOQ. As she walked in, she stopped at the desk and asked the young airman manning the desk, "Any messages for Jones?"

"Yes, ma'am," he replied politely, handing her a message pad. Tom had called; he wanted to meet her in the lobby at 1900 hours. A.J. proceeded to her room. It was pretty much like a decent motel room. There were two queen beds, two desks, and a couple chairs. The TV sat atop a long chest. The room appeared to be set up for two people, but for now, she didn't have a roommate. She had sent her fatigues to the cleaners upon arrival, underwear as well. That had been the weakness at the Global Petroleum camp. Their water for showers and washing clothes was well water, and it smelled as though it was only one step from petroleum. It was loaded with sulphur and seemed hard as hell. Their drinking water was trucked in from town and was marginally better.

The water at the BOQ here at Howard was fantastic. The shower felt strong enough to peel skin off, and the supply of hot water was endless.

When she got out and dried off, she looked in the dresser. *Let's see.* There was a pair of jeans, one black halter, and the dressy shirt she had been wearing when she left Manuel and Maria's. Everything else was either camo, fatigues, or had been blown up. Her shoes were good news/bad news. It was either sneakers or combat boots. Good news for comfort, but zero style points. Oh well, it was hardly like Tom would fire her.

She had little trouble killing time till 1845 hours. Walking to the lobby ate up a few, and just as she was about to sit on a couch in the lobby, Tom strode through the door. He was wearing a beard now with quite a bit of gray in it. The crew cut was gone, and he looked somewhat scruffy again, a lot like he had appeared in Cali.

"Are you ready, Miss Jones?"

"Yes, sir," she replied. He escorted her to an Air Force sedan. It was a very plain dark blue Ford with U.S. Air Force decals all over it.

"So how are you feeling, A.J.?"

"Getting better every day. It looks really ugly now, all purple and green and yellow, really gross. But that means it's healing. I don't need the pain pills very often, and I'm going to try the swimming stuff tomorrow."

"Sounds good. By the way, you need some clothes girl!"

"I had some clothes, Tom, but some ass blew them up! Hell, I had a TV, a laptop, lots of shit."

"Somebody that would do that needs to be put down like a rabid dog." Tom got quiet; he did that when he was thinking, "You know, we really do need to terminate him. He's insane and rich, and that's an extremely dangerous combination."

"Agreed. Got a plan?"

"No, and if I did, I'd be afraid to execute it. I've got a leak. It's very close to me, but I don't know who yet."

"Are you sure it's a leak? I mean you could just have a good bug somewhere."

"No, we've eliminated that. I think your brother might solve the mystery though. I gave him all the numbers of all the phones I use and all the people I call. Sooner or later his voice recognition algorithms are going to pay off. One good thing about the queen of spades deal is that T.D. says you are a very popular topic, and it gives him access to more conversations than he can read. He's having to get help from Stateside."

They pulled up to the Officers' Club. Tom used the valet parking and escorted A.J. inside and to a seat. He quickly ordered drinks, a Crown and water for each of them. While they were waiting for the waiter to return, Tom said, "A.J., you really need some more clothes."

"I know, you said that already, but I don't know how to get off base, and I don't have an ID, so I can't get in the PX."

"I'll have Nancy take you somewhere tomorrow."

"How do you know Nancy?"

"Did you really believe she was Air Force? Even in here, I still have a few people looking out for you. She's CIA. She's an analyst, but she's trained. I've got several people watching your back. Before we talk next time, I expect you to have made them all."

A.J. shook her head. She should have known. Maybe if it weren't for the pain meds. Uh oh. "Hey, Tom, don't let me drink much. I took a pain pill a few hours ago."

Tom nodded and smiled. Their drinks arrived. Tom declared a truce on shoptalk. He asked about getting to see her brother; he also made a point to let her know how much of an asset T.D. had been.

A.J. had gone all out. She had ordered a filet, baked potato, and salad, and of course another Crown Royal.

By the time she had eaten, she was experiencing a serious case of the nods.

"A.J., I'm taking you back to your quarters. I'm afraid you're already going to be asleep in the car. We'll talk some more tomorrow, okay?"

She nodded in a dreamy mood. Tom was right; he had to wake her up at the BOQ. At least she was able to wake up. She kissed Tom on the cheek and made her way to her room. Five minutes later, she was between the sheets and snoring.

Chapter 24

Panama City, Panama

"So, I guess Tom blew my cover, huh?" Nancy and A.J. were making the trip to Panama City to get some clothing for A.J. This time, she didn't need any "escort" clothing, just some day-to-day civvies and some better shoes. They intended to buy some local looking clothing as well so she didn't stand out as an American. Nancy had borrowed a plain Toyota sedan from the CIA's small fleet of cars.

"Yeah, Tom told me you were helping keep an eye out for me for safety reasons."

"So, you're pretty unpopular with someone?'

"You could say that. I guess I should probably get a wig too; I hate wearing them, they're hot and uncomfortable, but they do help with kinda keeping a low profile. The short hair stands out in this part of the world. Much as I hate them, I need some heels too."

"What does this Tom guy actually do, Anna? Or can you say?"

"Better not say, Nancy."

"That's fine, need to know, I get it."

A.J. had been giving Tom's intelligence leak some thought. They had discussed it at breakfast that morning. A.J. made a point of mentally cataloging what had been leaked and who had knowledge of those items. There wasn't a soul Tom could come up with. It was a real mystery. She had an idea. If she was right, it would be deeply upsetting to Tom, so she didn't plan to tell him, just in case she was wrong. The tip-off for her was that serious leaks hadn't occurred until Carlos had put a price on A.J.'s head. On the one hand, she was a little shocked Tom hadn't made the connection; but if she was right, there was a reason he ignored the possibility. Her plan would involve some outside assistance, but the first help she needed would be coming from T.D. That would keep her conspiracy very small, at least in the beginning. She would also need some help from Nancy, assuming she would cooperate.

"Nancy, I need a favor from you, maybe a couple."

"Sure, Anna, what do you need?"

"To begin with, a sat phone."

"I can do that, but why? All you're supposed to be doing is kicking back, recuperating."

"I know, but we have a problem. There's no reason I can't be working on it. Tell me something else; this is really top-secret shit. How much do you think you can help without saying anything to your people?"

"Well, I know I can swing the sat phone without saying anything. We have a few. I can log it out without saying I loaned it to you. What else?"

"I'm not sure yet."

The two were headed back toward Balboa and the base. A.J. was getting her radar back operating again.

"Hey, the two guys in the car behind us… they've been hanging back all day in Panama City. Are you going to introduce us sometime?"

"Oh, shit, if I do, they're really going to get their asses chewed. They're part of your security detail, but you weren't supposed to know. When did you make them?"

"In the city. When I was trying on a swimsuit, I saw the same little airman from behind the desk at the BOQ in civvies watching me when I checked out the suit in the mirror. After that I saw him and his bud in eating in the restaurant we had lunch in."

"I guess I'll pull them aside and tell them they need to work on their Klingon cloaking devices."

"Are you armed, Nancy?"

"Yeah, that's why I wore the skirt. It's strapped to my leg."

"Thought so, I've had to wear one there too. Makes you walk a little funny. It works better at night in a crowded place though."

Nancy laughed. "Okay, I'll keep that in mind."

A.J. walked into her room with her arms loaded with bags. Nancy had promised to return in a few minutes with the sat phone. She went over the beginnings of her plan while she waited. There was another item she would need, and Nancy had said that wouldn't be a problem either. She needed a recorder with a phone pickup.

Once Nancy had dropped off the equipment, A.J. placed her first call. The recorder was connected to the sat phone; every call would be recorded while her plan unwound. She checked the phone to make sure she had a signal and dialed Kevin back at the Global camp. Luckily, she had an ability to remember numbers, all kinds. It was a little creepy, but really handy with phone numbers. Kevin came up on line quickly.

"Hey, Kevin, it's A.J."

"Missing us already, A.J.? Are you ready to come back?"

She laughed. "Soon, Kevin, soon. Listen, I'm working on some stuff. Think you could have T.D. call me? I want to go over some programs on the new laptop he fixed up for me."

"Sure, be glad to. Seriously, how do you feel?"

"Sore, but better every day. Swimming and piña coladas work miracles. There's something else. This is just between you and me. Nobody, and I mean nobody, can know about this. Okay?"

"Sounds serious, but okay. Is T.D. included in the nobody category?"

"Yes, absolutely freakin' nobody."

"Wow, okay, shoot."

"I've got something really important I'm working on. It's possible I may need some backup. If I needed them, could I get some of the operators away from you? Just for a couple days, but they'd need to be able to get out-of-country, and with little or no notice. Oh, and they'd need some hardware."

She could almost hear the wheels spinning in Kevin's head. "Maybe. I'll need to do some checking. Anybody in particular?"

"I know Pete and Cal best, so one of them if it's possible. I trust all of them, and they're all good, so it's up to you."

"Could this blow up in our faces?"

"Maybe, but if it works, we could be the shit. No risk, no reward, right?"

"I guess. I'll have T.D. call you. This number?"

"Yeah, I don't need this tapped."

"Okay, will do. Later." The static came up, and she ended the call. She re-played the recorder. It had done fine.

Ten minutes later, the sat phone came up with its chirping ring. Her brother had returned her call. "What's up, sis?"

"I'm working on some stuff. I want to send you some sound files of telephone conversations that I'm gonna be taping. I don't want to send the tapes. Can I run them through the laptop and get them to you somehow?"

"Shit! Yes, it can be done. It's a shame we're not in the States."

"Why?"

"In the States, if you could get to a military base or a university, you could send it to me over the internet. But with me here, no way. You'll have to get an adapter to go from the recorder to the microphone plug on the laptop. Then you'll have to pull up a program I put in there called MP1. Once you've saved the file, burn it to a floppy, and send it to me here. Don't expect instant service. I can encode the files here, but I'll have to feed them to Fort Meade NSA when I get a satellite pass. Each voice needs thirty seconds or so, and each one needs to be a separate file, okay?"

"Got it, I think. What's the internet?"

"Don't worry, you'll be hearing all about it in a year or two; in fact, I'll give you some stocks you need to buy. Load up on them and you'll be richer than our mom."

"Nobody's richer than Mom." She laughed.

"So true. What are you wanting with the voice comparisons?"

"I want to know if any of them have come up in any conversations with any cowboys."

"Holy shit! Okay, you aren't doing anything I need to worry about, are you? I was just getting used to not having to think about you getting in trouble."

"I'm being good, T.D. I'm on an Air Force base, and Tom has several CIA bodyguards watching me, supposedly without my knowledge."

"So you've already made them?"

"Yeah, made them today while I was out buying clothes. Listen, I'll be back in touch T.D. I'm tired. I'm going to take a pain pill and go to bed."

"Ten-four, sis. Later."

Chapter 25

Howard AFB

Balboa, Panama

A.J. had just finished her laps in the pool at the officers' club and was drying off when Nancy showed up. She and A.J. lay down in a pair of loungers. It was about 0900 hours.

"Had breakfast yet?"

"No, I was up pretty late working on my special project."

"How's it coming?"

"Really just getting underway, but I got most of the preliminary stuff done. I start in earnest today."

"Are you going to leave the BOQ today?"

"Not sure, do I need to call you and check in?"

"Well, we don't want you to feel like you're a prisoner, but it would make it easier for us to keep an eye on you. Would you mind?"

"No, I understand, have you got a cell or a pager?"

Nancy nodded and pulled a card out of her purse. She jotted two numbers on the back and handed it to A.J. She looked at them and handed the card back to Nancy.

"You don't need the card?"

"Nah, I've got it."

"Need anything else?"

"Just a ride back to the BOQ if you brought a car."

"No problem, Anna."

A.J broke for lunch two hours later. She had called Manuel, she had called Maria, she had even called Amanda Jernigan, the JAG captain that had represented her during her Article 32 hearing just as an outside chance. With anyone who spoke Spanish, she had made sure she broke into Spanish in case that had an impact on the NSA program. She had tried Isobel's cell, but it had gone straight to voicemail, and A.J. didn't have another number for her.

The dining hall in the BOQ had a buffet line, and she had grabbed a salad and sandwich. She returned to her room and began turning all the calls into files on her laptop. About 1430 hours her desk phone rang. She hooked the pickup on the recorder and answered. "Yes?"

"Miss Jones, this is the front desk. You have a visitor in the lobby. We have instructions not to allow anyone up without your knowledge. Can you come down and verify you know her?"

Well, I wonder who could know I'm here? A quick look in the mirror verified she looked decent. She went to her bedside table, pulled out the .22 pistol and, after verifying it had one in the chamber, tucked it in the waistband of her jeans and headed downstairs. She walked in the lobby to see a familiar face; it was Isobel!

"Hello, Anna! How are you?" Isobel smiled and ran to hug A.J.

"Whoa! Please! No hugging." A.J. kissed her on the cheek instead. "I'll explain upstairs, c'mon up."

Isobel grabbed a small piece of carry-on luggage and followed her up. When they arrived, Isobel dropped her luggage and said, "Can I use your bathroom, Anna? I'm about to pop!"

"Sure!" A.J. replied. When Isobel closed the door, A.J. had a thought and grabbed the recorder. She turned it on and shoved it under the bed. Hopefully it would pick up. When Isobel came out, A.J. said, "I had actually tried to call you today. It went straight to voicemail. How did you ever find me? I'm supposed to be hidden to the world."

"Tom, of course. I had some time off coming, and he thought you might need company. I know why you didn't want a hug too, but honestly I forgot. How are you?"

"Pretty good actually, bored as hell. I went clothes shopping the other day; wish you had been here. You heard I guess what happened to all the beautiful stuff you helped me pick out in Puerto Vallarta?"

"Yeah, Tom said you pissed off the wrong person, and he blew up your whole building! Thank God you weren't home! By the way, Tom's coming in tomorrow. I'm supposed to ask you if you'd like to go fishing again."

"Sure, why not? It's not like I've got plans." A.J laughed. Actually she was a little pissed. Why would Tom tell anybody that didn't *need* to know where she was? Not that Isobel wasn't fun, but still. "Want to go to dinner tonight? Maybe the officers' club?"

"Think we can get in?"

"Oh, I hadn't thought about that. I've been, but with Tom. Let me check." A.J. picked up her desk phone and asked about being able to get in the club. The young man at the desk hemmed and hawed a little, but then said he could get them temporary passes. His tone of voice and mannerisms pretty much confirmed he was another of A.J.'s "guards." *Oh well, that's three; maybe Tom will be satisfied.* She turned to Isobel. "Well, that's done. We can get in."

"Yummy! No lounge lizards tonight, girlfriend; we'll have some primo single male companionship to pick from tonight!"

"Honestly, Isobel, do you ever think about anything but men?"

"No, really, I don't think so. Okay, yes I do. I've been thinking about you. What have you been doing besides getting shot?"

"I really don't think I could tell you. It's all been cloak and dagger stuff." She went to sit down in one of the chairs when she noticed the .22 poking her butt. She pulled it out and returned it to the bedside table.

"Damn, you're the real thing, aren't you! Have you used that?"

"Maybe, maybe not. Let's talk about something else."

"Deal! Show me the clothes you bought then. I want to see if I approve! You did buy some heels, didn't you?"

Pacific Ocean
Twenty-five Miles Offshore

A.J. was sitting in the fighting chair on the boat getting some rays. She had on her new bikini, but to keep from grossing anyone out, she had a plain white tee shirt on as well. Tom and Isobel had insisted on seeing her chest, so she had given them a peek. Sure enough, Isobel was grossed out, and Tom shook his head and looked pissed off.

"A.J., you should have been out of that tree way before anybody could get a make on your location."

"Hindsight's twenty-twenty. I had a job to do, or my team was gonna have a lot more company than they were equipped to handle."

"I guess. Kevin spoke very highly of your performance."

Isobel jumped in. "Enough shop talk, you two. Are we gonna fish and drink or not!"

Tom slapped Isobel on the ass and laughed. "She's right, you know. Let's get with the program!" They did.

The fishing was only fair that day. During the return trip Tom was smoking his traditional cigar, Isobel was topless and flirting with the crew, and A.J. was thoughtful. "Tom, I want a vacation."

"Well sure, A.J. I mean you deserve it. Where did you want to go?"

"I don't know, Tom, just out of here."

"When would you go?"

"Soon, today's Sunday. Could I leave Friday? I'll stay this week and work on getting better, and then I'm gone. I'll call you when I get wherever."

"What's this, Anna? You're leaving?" Isobel was suddenly serious.

"Yeah, I've just got to get away for awhile."

Tom looked A.J. in the eye. "A.J., I'm not your jailer. I just want to know wherever you are you're safe."

"I know. I'm working on a plan, one that will keep me safe. Besides, you know as well as I do I'm a threat to the people around me too."

They arrived back at the dock after a two-hour ride. When Tom and Isobel dropped A.J. at the BOQ, Isobel ran up to A.J.'s room long enough to grab her carry-on bag. She kissed A.J. on the cheek.

"Tom's got meetings in Panama City for several days. He's got a suite. Sorry, girl, but you know me; I love a suite. Shopping, clubs, I love you, Anna, but I'm going with Tom. We'll get together before you escape, I promise. Adios!"

The truth was A.J. was not really sorry to see Isobel go. They were very, very different. Isobel was a blast, but A.J. had decided she was best experienced in small doses. Besides, she still had to transfer the tape of Isobel to a file and get the floppy to her brother. The desk looked into it, and actually UPS was the fastest way to get the disc to T.D. He would have it Tuesday morning. She pulled Kevin up on the sat phone when she returned to her room.

"How about it, Kevin? Can you get me some backup?"

"You are a very large pain in the ass, A.J., but yes. How soon do you need them?"

"I'd say either this week or not at all, Kevin. I kind of put the bait in the water. I let word out today about something that should force someone's hand. Can they be here in twenty-four hours?"

"I'll call you back. Stay close to the phone. Out."

Her plan was set in motion. The next move would belong to someone else. Kevin called back at 2200 hours. He had been able to put transportation together. Between a Global chopper and an Air Force C-130, Cal and two more operators would arrive in Balboa in roughly twenty-four hours. The C-130 had greatly reduced the complications involved in travelling with automatic weapons. Delta really frowned on that.

A.J. got a shower and lay down. As her head hit the pillow, she had an uncomfortable thought. Her dad had always said never walk in a room without an exit strategy. Right now, she had no idea what that would be.

Chapter 26

Howard AFB

Balboa, Panama

Monday and Tuesday seemed to crawl by. A.J. was ready for this to be over, one way or the other. She swam, did some slow and easy workouts at the gym, and forced herself to do some light runs. It hurt, no question about it, but she seemed to be improving rapidly.

Tuesday afternoon she had completed her list. She picked up the phone and called Nancy. “Hey, Nancy. It’s Anna.”

“So what’s up, Anna? Are you going somewhere, or do you need another favor?”

“The latter I’m afraid, Nancy.”

“Okay, I was afraid of that. What now?”

A.J. rattled off the list; a motel for Cal and the guys, a car, a panel van, and two items that caused Nancy to go into a mixture of shock and disbelief.

"Okay, I can halfway understand the motel and vehicles. Those alone are probably enough to get me suspended without pay for not telling my supervisor, but what the fuck? A dart gun and a respirator? You are one sick bitch or a genius, most likely both. And curare? Where the hell am I supposed to get that? And, worse, what in the hell are you going to do with it?"

"It's Central America, Nancy. The stories are the natives use it left and right, no? As far as what I'm going to do with it, best you don't know right now. Oh, one more thing. I know your neck is stretched way out here. If this goes well, you're going to get a very positive performance review. If it goes south, well, I can pay you for the month or so you'd be suspended. Blame it on me; I threatened you. You're CIA, you're trained to lie, aren't you?"

"I have a feeling I'm going to regret this, but I'm going to do it, assuming I can find all this. Who's going to be in the motel?"

"I've got three contract operators I worked with in Colombia coming in tonight. No offense, but I know these guys. I took a bullet for them; they'll do the same for me. I don't know that about your guys. Besides, no telling who'll talk. I know these guys won't."

"Okay. I'm sure I'll regret it, but I'm in. When I say I'm in, I mean it. I'll do this, but you're including me in the action. I've got no field experience. If I'm gonna take an ass chewing, I want to have ridden the bull. Are we clear?"

"Okay, I'll include you in the op, but I'm not taking you into a shooting situation. I wouldn't be able to live with myself. You can help, but you're support, okay?"

Tuesday afternoon, Cal called A.J.'s sat phone. "A.J., we're on the ground. What in the hell are you up to?"

"I'm playing a hunch. Tom has a leak, a serious one. I think I know who it is, but my plan is going to have to play out. I'm going to have a CIA chick pick you up. She'll put you up in a motel. I need you guys ready to move on a moment's notice and loaded for bear. I can't tell you the plan until this begins to develop. If this works, we'll be heroes. If not, well, I guess you can blame it on me."

"It's okay. You know we're on your team. Anything for the queen!"

A.J. laughed. "I hope this shit works, I really do. Call me back when Nancy has you in place. I don't want to risk being seen with you. I need everybody thinking I'm here on my own. Call me back, out."

Wednesday morning dawned cloudy and windy. The day seemed to fit A.J.'s mood. She knew something would happen soon, but the how and when were something out of her control. She felt tense. Strange, when she knew the score, she felt amazingly calm, even when facing potential danger. At this point, she had no clue of the score. She didn't even know what game was being played. Then it came to her; chess. Unfortunately right now, she could see only her side of the board. She needed another viewpoint. She knew exactly who to call.

"What's up, sis?"

"I wish I knew. I feel like I'm playing a dangerous game with no rules."

"That's exactly what you're doing, A.J. You're supposed to be doing nothing. You should get the hell out of Dodge and leave this to someone else."

"I'd love to. But unless we settle this, people are going to die."

"Agreed. You realize this game you're playing means one of those people could be you. You're up to something.

I don't know what it is, but I know it's happening. And I know you've decided not to tell me about it. Why is that?"

"I didn't want to worry you. I need your thought processes to not be clouded by worrying about me. I can separate these things; you can't. I know you."

"Too late for that, sis. You called me. What do you want?"

"Okay, you're right. Did you get the voice files?"

"Yes. I massaged them and uploaded them to Fort Meade. They'll be running them through the computers there."

"Know anything else? Anything out of the ordinary?"

"Affirmative on that too. Carlos got some calls this week. Then he completely dropped off the grid. That's very unusual. We were pretty sure he was in Cali up until the showdown at the airport. We were basing that on phone intercepts as well as human intelligence from agents Tom has. Now, poof! He's completely disappeared. Wanna know where I think he is?"

"Absolutely!"

"I think he's headed to Panama, and I think my twisted sister knows why. What are you doing, A.J.?"

"I'm trying to force Carlos to make a mistake, but I need feedback. Tell me about Carlos's phone calls, who is he talking to, what he's saying?"

"Okay. What I ought to do is tell you I'm not saying shit until you come clean with me. On the other hand, I've got to help you. You and I are going to have a serious discussion. Since Monday, we have Carlos talking several times to a known associate we believe to be Roberto. Roberto had been in Cartagena. He left for Panama on a commercial flight. He had a different passport, but a DEA source ID'd him at the airport. Carlos got a few more calls from Roberto Monday night from a payphone we were able to trace to Panama. Then Carlos went off the grid."

"But what were they saying?"

"They're using a simple substitution code. They know we may be listening. But they keep talking about 'solving the problem.' I can tell you this; they're both laughing and looking forward to it. Carlos dropped one hint. He says if they do this, it solves his problem while saving him a lot of money. So, what does that tell you?"

"Not a lot," she lied. "Tell me this, does Carlos have contacts in Panama?"

"We don't think so, not that we know about anyway."

"Okay. Damn, I wish I had a lot more intel. I'm going to have to make this up on the fly. Thanks, T.D. I'll call you every day."

"You better."

The game moved to the next phase with the sound of her room phone ringing.

"Yes?"

"Miss Jones, there's a package here at the front desk for you."

"Okay, I'll be right down." A thought came to her. "Who delivered it?"

"A guy in an Air Force uniform."

"Okay, I'll be right there." She went to the lobby quickly. It was a manila envelope, addressed to Anna Jones. A.J. walked to a chair and sat down. There wasn't much in it, a handwritten note addressed to "Anna" and a Polaroid. The photo took her breath away. The quality was poor, the lighting bad, but there was no doubt; it was Isobel. She was seated in a heavy metal chair. She appeared to be nude. Her hands were duct taped to the chair arms. A copy of that morning's *La Justicia* newspaper was propped in her lap. Duct tape covered her mouth, but her pleading eyes spoke volumes. Isobel's upper body was secured to the chair with barbed wire, wrapped round and round. A.J. felt a brief wave of nausea wash over her. She opened the note. It was handwritten in Spanish.

Anna – as you can see, I have your friend. If you ever hope to see her alive, call me at this number within an hour. I look forward to meeting you in person. Carlos

She peered into the envelope to see if she had missed anything. She held the envelope upside down and shook it lightly. A card fluttered out, landing on the light blue-carpeted floor. She picked it up, turning it over. It was a queen of spades.

She walked quickly to the desk. "The man who brought this, what did he look like?"

"Just a guy, a sergeant."

A.J. thought for a moment. "Do you have surveillance tapes of the lobby? Anything?"

"Sure, we have the lobby camera and one outside."

"Cue them up, now!"

"Ma'am, I'm not sure—"

A.J. grabbed him by the shirt. "Listen, Corporal Atkins, or whatever your real name is, this is important. Lives are at stake. Get your ass back there and cue up the freakin' tapes. Got it?"

"Yes, ma'am. Follow me."

The two walked to a small room behind the desk. A single Sony monitor displayed six views, the lobby, the outside entry, and the elevator landings on the four floors of the BOQ. The young man pushed buttons on the VCR until it began playing jerky motions in reverse. Atkins stopped the tape. "Okay, that's him, getting out of the Jeep."

A.J. watched the tape intently, her mind whirling with possible moves and counter-moves. The quality of the tape was poor, and the man was wearing a cap obscuring a lot of his face. When he entered, she looked at the view from the desk camera. Average height, average build, but it could be Roberto, with a clean shave and a crew cut. She watched as he spoke briefly to Atkins and handed him the envelope. The man never looked up. It seemed he knew where the camera was. There… finally! When he turned to leave, it was there, nearly hidden by his collar, but there. He had what appeared to be half of a scorpion tattoo on his neck. His collar nearly hid it, but not entirely. Roberto had one in the same place.

"Do you work with Nancy?" A.J. asked the corporal.

He nodded.

"Call her, I need her here ASAP. Tell her it's begun. Look at the Jeep again and check with the main gate. See how he got in here and do it now." A.J. paced, and then she sat down and looked at the Polaroid again. Something bothered her about it, but she wasn't able to see the problem. Isobel's chair seemed to be in a darkened room, under a single light source. There was nothing in the background and a plain concrete floor in the foreground. There just wasn't much to go on.

She pulled out the note again and had just begun to look it over again when Atkins told her she had a phone call. He pointed to a white phone by the elevator.

She picked it up when it rang and simply answered, "This is Anna."

"Anna, Tom. Have you heard from Isobel?"

"No," she lied, "should I?"

"I don't know. She said she was going out for a drink last night in the hotel bar. I went down to have one with her after an hour or so, and she wasn't there. She never came back to the room."

"Well, you know Isobel, Tom. There's no telling." Lying to Tom was distasteful, but she wasn't ready to bring him into her game.

"Okay, if you hear from her, call me please." She could hear concern in his voice. They were an item. A.J. had been suspicious almost from the beginning, but Tom's tone of voice verified her opinion almost as certainly as an outright admission.

"I will." With that, they exchanged goodbyes. A.J. had just hung up the phone when she turned to see Nancy coming in the door in jeans and a shirt.

"What's going on, Anna?" she asked.

"Carlos is going on, Nancy. He has Isobel." A.J. handed Nancy the envelope and looked at her watch. "I have thirty minutes to call him back. I put out the bait, and he took it. Now we see if the fish or the angler wins this."

Nancy looked at the contents of the envelope. "Shit! Okay, I wish we could go back to my building, but there's no time." She turned to Atkins. "Get our deputy station chief on the line, Ted. Tell him to put our team on hot alert, and Anna's team as well. She's going to make a call from here to this number in a few minutes. It's a cell. They need to see if they can tell what tower it pings off." Nancy handed the note to Atkins, pointing to the number. "Put us in the break room with two phones and find me an area map too." She looked at A.J. "Well, it's time to get to work. You set this deal up. Time to finish it."

Chapter 27

Howard Air Force Base
Balboa, Panama
Wednesday, 1015 hours

"Greetings, Miss DeJesus, or should I call you queen?" Carlos had answered in Spanish.

"Entirely up to you, Carlos. You wanted me to call?" A.J.'s voice no doubt conveyed her disgust. She and Nancy were seated at a table in the break room. Nancy was listening to the call on an extension with one ear and to her lead techie back at the CIA annex in Panama City on another phone. A map of the greater Panama City area lay on the table between them. A.J.'s tape recorder was running.

"Yes, Anna. I'm looking forward to meeting you in person. There has been much unpleasantness between us. I was hoping we could settle our disagreements."

"I imagine you would like that, Carlos. Look, we both know you want me dead. That's fine, because I feel the same about you. You really shouldn't have taken Isobel. I sent you a message in Cartagena. I warned you, you should disappear, or I told you I would kill your men then your mistresses then your family. You've lost many men. Are you stupid?"

"No, Queen of Spades, I'm not stupid; I'm crazy. You have been an expensive *puta* to me. Since you arrived in Colombia, I've lost many, many men. You stole my brother, my money, and my drugs. Worst, you have cost me much honor, *puta*. I was prepared to pay a million dollars U.S. to have you killed, but, since I am crazy, I've decided I want to kill you myself."

"Carlos, my condolences for your losses. We agree; we want to see each other dead, so let's get on with it. Let Isobel go. We can meet and settle this, man to bitch, no?" Nancy stared at A.J., her eyes wide. While Nancy had no training in hostage negotiations, she was confident this *wasn't* how it was done. "So, Carlos, how do we resolve this?"

"I will give you directions to a meeting spot. You will meet one of my men there. He will bring you to me, and we will settle this. If you do this for me, I will free your friend. I will return her to you whether you meet me or not." *What does he mean by that?* "Yes, *puta*, if you do as I say, I will release her. If you don't, I will still return her to you, one piece at a time."

"I'm sure you would. But, as you said, you're crazy. Why should I come to you? How do I know you won't just kill both of us?"

A.J.'s mind spun. There was no easy answer, but she thought she actually had the upper hand. He *was* crazy, and she wasn't.

"You have my word." *Yeah, right!* "So, Anna, you will meet my man?"

Nancy shook her head.

"Yes, Carlos. Where? And when?"

"Be waiting on the front steps of the Hotel Riande Granada in an hour. My man will find you and bring you to me." Nancy shoved a note to A.J. *No, hell no. Tell him you'll meet him at Solo Restaurante. It's next door.*

"No, Carlos, I'm not crazy or stupid. I stand on the steps while some cowboy drives by, puts a bullet in my head, and collects a million? Not happening, Carlos. I'll meet your man in Solo Restaurante next door. And I need two hours, not one." Carlos erupted in a tirade of curses. A.J. let him rant for a while. "Well, Señor Scorpion?"

"Very well, two hours, Solo Restaurante. Remember, *puta*, I can start cutting fingers off your friend any time after that."

"I remember, asshole. I'm looking forward to meeting you."

"Come alone, Anna."

"Tell your man the same, Carlos. This is about you and me." A.J. hung up the phone and turned to Nancy. "Well? What can you tell me?"

"Give my techie a few minutes. I'll have a small team near the restaurant in fifteen minutes. You're not going in there alone."

"I don't intend to. I need Cal and the dart gun handy. Whoever Carlos's contact is, I need him darted and in the van. Any of Carlos's men that show up, eliminate them."

Nancy looked at Anna; she hadn't heard someone be quite so blunt. The second phone rang. Nancy answered, listened, and turned to A.J.

"We did get some hits on his phone, but we think they aren't worth a whole lot. He showed up on three different towers, so he was probably moving. We can only pin him down to a general area. He's somewhere around the canal."

"Okay, we'll deal with it." A.J. dressed in jeans, a halter, and a cotton long-sleeve shirt. Sneakers seemed most appropriate, so on they went. She and Nancy left the BOQ and met Cal and his two men as well as the two bodyguards that had been helping Nancy.

"We've got the van and the dart gun you wanted," Cal told her. "What exactly do you have planned?"

"I'll meet him in the restaurant. I need one person inside, just to yell for help if I give the sign. I'd suggest Nancy. I'm sure Carlos's guy won't be alone. He'll have a couple more with him. Most likely in a vehicle waiting outside. Someone needs to arrest them for double parking, anything, for the time being. Whenever Carlos's man and I exit the restaurant, you guys will dart him. We'll load him in the van, and I'll get it from there. After I get Isobel's location, we go after her. Questions? Comments?"

Nancy spoke up. "How do you plan to get this guy to give up Isobel's location?"

"You don't want to know, Nancy." A.J. looked her in the eyes. Nancy could see a flash of anger she hadn't seen before.

Cal spoke. "So we'll have to figure out the takedown at the site where he's holding Isobel on the fly?"

"Yes. And I suggest unless we see a way we can just grab Isobel and go, we take down any security and then let me go in against Carlos."

"Alone?" asked Cal.

"Alone, or at least giving the appearance of alone. Don't get me wrong. I'm fine having backup, but he's crazy. If he concentrates on me, he'll make a mistake, I'm positive he will."

Cal looked at A.J. "I hope you know what you're doing. I know Tom wanted to take Carlos down, but somehow I suspect you've baited him to come for you. That's brave, or stupid."

"Or both," Nancy said. "What's with the A.J. stuff, Anna?"

"A.J.'s what I prefer to answer to. Since I've been working with Tom, I've had so many passports and names I can hardly keep up. These guys"—she punched Cal in the arm—"are my brothers-in-arms. We've taken fire together. To them, I'm A.J. To others, I'm what Tom wants me to be."

"Do you mind if I call you A.J. then?"

A.J. almost grinned. "No, that's fine. How long do we have left?"

Nancy looked at her watch. "We've got about an hour left."

Cal broke the meeting up. "Final checks on everything, guys. I want us to be in place as early as possible to watch for anybody working for Carlos. We leave as soon as we can do radio checks. We especially need Nancy to have good com. She's A.J.'s lifeline. A.J., are you taking a weapon in the restaurant?"

"Hell yes, I'm taking the nine."

"Okay, good. You haven't completely lost your mind then. One more thing. I don't know what they taught you in boot camp, but avoid hand-to-hand combat at all costs. It's nothing like the movies. If you don't end the fight in five to ten seconds, you've already lost."

A.J. nodded and turned to walk away.

Solo Restaurante
1210 hours

Nancy walked in the restaurant and took a seat offering what seemed to be the best visibility. She had selected her best "local" outfit. She had training to look invisible with the agency and was fairly proficient at it. Her large straw bag was excellent for concealing a firearm. Nancy had been issued a Beretta 9 mm, and she could perforate the hell out of a paper target. So far, there had been no need to use it as intended.

As her eyes adjusted to the low light, she looked around. She saw quite a few people, but no men, or women for that matter, seated alone. That changed a few moments later as the man A.J. had identified as Roberto came in. He paused to look around the dining area prior to selecting a secluded booth. The man set a cell phone down on the table in front of him.

Nancy listened to her earpiece as she watched Roberto. She heard her CIA crew quietly report taking down the vehicle Roberto had arrived in; two occupants were detained. The vehicle was left by the curb, and a tracking device had been installed under the rear bumper. Likewise, Cal's crew had taken a woman into custody who had just looked wrong. She was carrying an Uzi in her straw bag. *So far so good.*

A.J. entered the room. After allowing a moment or two to adjust to the light, she located Roberto. She walked to his table and sat opposite him in the booth. She watched Roberto put his phone back in his pocket as she sat. Apparently he was checking in.

"So, Roberto, you are my escort to Carlos?"

He prepared a cigar as he answered, "Yes, Anna, or A.J. Which do you prefer?"

"It only matters when someone important to me is speaking Roberto, so, it's your choice."

"What if I prefer bitch?" He blew a smoke ring in her face.

"It makes no difference to me."

"Are you alone, Anna?"

"Of course, are you?"

"Yes. Well, we should be going. I have to bring you to Carlos."

"I know. You're looking forward to it, aren't you?"

"Of course. Yes, we want you dead, but we may take our time. Besides, I'm sure Isobel wants to be released. So, let's go." Roberto quietly slid a pair of handcuffs to A.J. "Put these on, behind your back. I understand you are capable of much mayhem in a vehicle."

A.J. thought about making a move for about a second. Roberto had her by seventy pounds and six inches in height. She had no advantage of surprise, and she could plainly see Nancy, so technically, she felt she still controlled the situation. She did as she was told and put one cuff on her right wrist and then attached the second cuff behind her back. Roberto stood and walked to her side of the booth and helped her to her feet. He picked up her straw bag and looked inside. He smiled as he removed the Beretta.

"I knew you wouldn't show up without a weapon." Roberto dropped the clip into the bag and cleared the weapon. He looked into the bag and saw a wrap. "Here, señorita, let me put your wrap over your shoulders. It will keep you from looking like you've been arrested." He took her arm and walked her out of the restaurant after throwing some money on the table.

"How chivalrous, Roberto, I had no idea."

Roberto walked her outside and turned left. He proceeded down the sidewalk until he arrived in front of a white Toyota. He seemed puzzled.

"Is there a problem, Roberto? You assured me you were alone. Carlos gave his word you would be alone." She was staring deep into his eyes when she heard the noise; it sounded like someone slapping skin. The small, red dart appeared on Roberto's neck at the same instant.

"Shit! What was that?" Roberto released A.J.'s arm and ran his hand to his neck. His eyes widened as he realized he'd been darted. "What have you done, bitch? You'll never see your slut friend alive now!" Roberto reached under his shirt for a large knife, but just as it cleared his scabbard, Cal's large arms wrapped Roberto up.

"Well, looks like we both lied about being alone, huh? Quickly guys, get him to the van. Does anyone have a key to these?" She showed off the cuffs. Nancy walked to her. She had a key.

By the time A.J. climbed into the rear of the van, Roberto was lying on the floor face up with his hands and feet duct taped. He was breathing in shallow little gasps.

"Bet you're wondering what was in the dart, huh, Roberto?" Roberto nodded rapidly. "You should be familiar with the toxin, my friend. It's called curare. Do you know how it works?" Roberto shook his head. "C'mon, you should know this. Geez. South American natives use it in their blowguns. They dart food, like a monkey. The toxin paralyzes the diaphragm. No diaphragm, no air going in or out. Kinda like you right now, Ricardo. Then the monkey passes out, falls out of the tree, and the natives have dinner." She stared at Ricardo as his eyelids began to flicker.

"A.J., what are you doing? You can't do this!"

"Bullshit, Nancy, I haven't got time to play games with him. We need to know where Isobel is. You wanna feel good about yourself? Take the respirator and bring him back. Better hurry, he's only got about another three, four minutes before brain damage starts. Go! Do it, give him shots until he comes around." Nancy pushed the respirator to Ricardo's face. They watched his rib cage rise and fall with the respirator's shots of oxygen. In just a few moments, his color came back. His eyes came into focus, and when they did, he was looking directly into A.J.'s eyes.

"Okay, let's try this again. Where's Isobel?" Ricardo blurted with outgoing air after every time Nancy applied the respirator to his face.

"I…can't…tell…you…that…Carlos…will…kill…me. "

A.J. pulled the respirator away and leaned down until her nose was nearly touching Carlos's. "Do you think I won't? Six minutes, Ricardo, that's all it takes. Six minutes with no respirator and you're dead. You just did three. Tell you what. Let's try four this time." She made an exaggerated motion of throwing the respirator aside. Ricardo shook his head back and forth, gulping like a fish.

After about two minutes, his eyelids flickered, and his lips began to turn blue.

Ten minutes later, A.J. and Cal were in Roberto's Toyota, and the remainder of the group was in a truck headed for an abandoned oil terminal in the area between the U.S. embassy and the canal. Ricardo had been dropped at the CIA station on the way and currently had a ventilator down his throat and was missing his shirt. According to the literature, his diaphragm would begin working again in less than eight hours.

Cal looked at A.J. "Remind me not to piss you off. He gave it all up. How many guys are there, where they're supposed to be, and he doesn't have a mark on him. That third time, I've never seen anyone more afraid in my life. You're a real bitch, A.J."

"No, I'm the Queen of Spades."

Chapter 28

Abandoned Oil Terminal

Miraflores Lock, Panama Canal

1330 hours

Just as the large, rusty above-ground tanks of the oil terminal Roberto had described came into sight, Cal suddenly pulled off the road. The truck with the CIA operators did the same.

"I've given it a some of thought. It's not dark. We need to get to wherever they have Isobel in broad daylight. That means we have to get close enough to surprise the guards totally. Roberto said one or two at the gate, right?" A.J. nodded. "Okay, one of the CIA guys needs to drive Roberto's car. Until we're right up next to him, he could pass for Roberto, especially wearing his shirt. You need to sit upfront, holding your arms behind you. You're cuffed, remember?"

"So we take him down at the gate?"

"Yeah. If there's only one, maybe we can take him down without killing him; if not…" He shrugged.

"So, the second vehicle lays back. Ricardo had two guys in the car, make one of them you and be holding a gun to my head. If you have to shoot, you shoot him."

Cal continued, thinking aloud, "Okay, that gets us in the gate. Ricardo says two buildings; a shop, which is where the Polaroid was taken and a two-story office. Any ideas?"

A.J. bounced back with, "Yeah, two buildings. Let's see, we're through the gate, and the other truck hangs back. If anybody's outside, we drive up to the warehouse, and we sit until they get ten, twenty meters away. Two of you guys drag me out. I'll put up a fight, and then you guys take 'em down. At that point, we call in the second vehicle. Ricardo says five guys, but they've got to sleep. I'm betting somebody's sleeping in the office. Isobel's probably in the warehouse."

"How do you know?"

"Are you crazy? Of course I don't know. What I do know is if we wait long enough to have enough people to do it right, he'll know something isn't right; we'll lose both Isobel and Carlos."

"Okay, like you said, it sucks, but it's what we've got. Give me a few to brief everybody and we'll go. You ready?"

"Yep. Wait, no I'm not. Actually, I've gotta pee."

Cal laughed. "I wondered. The Queen is human after all. Okay, hide behind the car door while we talk." Somehow A.J. found humor too. *Strange what was funny in life and death situations.*

The Toyota pulled into a narrow spot in the row of trees lining the service road that ran parallel to the canal. A worn, decomposing sign announced they were at Amoco Terminal 28.

A single guard with an AK slung over his shoulder sauntered toward the Toyota on A.J.'s side. He leaned forward to get a look at the famous Queen of Spades. The guard looked up at "Ricardo" and saw nothing but the end of a large suppressor pointed directly at his nose. When he tried to back away, A.J.'s supposedly bound hands grabbed him by the neck, pulling him so close to the car he couldn't get to the AK. Cal exited the back seat in a flash. A few moments later the guard watched the Toyota pull through the gate, his hands and feet zip tied and duct taped to a tree.

The asphalt drive made a gentle ninety-degree sweep coming into a large paved apron between the buildings. One guard was visible, sitting on the porch of what looked like the office building. He stood and walked toward the car, AK-47 in his hands.

Cal tapped the driver on the shoulder. "Stop here, make him come to us. Time to put up a fight, A.J." With that, Cal jumped out of the back seat at the same time the driver exited. Cal threw A.J.'s door open, grabbed her by the hair, and dragged her out of the car. Holding her wrists together behind her back, she kneed him near the balls and was rewarded with a backhand across the face; she went down to her knees. The guard, transfixed by the queen getting her ass kicked, never noticed the pistol in the driver's hand until the suppressed weapon spit a single 9 mm round. The guard died instantly when the round entered his forehead.

A.J. pulled the tape off her mouth. "Anybody see any more guards?" Nobody did. That smelled wrong to A.J., but considering Carlos was crazy, and he could be napping, snorting, or using Isobel, it might be okay. "Let's bring in the other guys, okay?"

Cal agreed and called them in. He told the other man with him in the Toyota to check the windows in the office. A.J. could see the man indicating there were occupants. Cal quietly waved him back and waited until the truck with the rest of their meager forces arrived.

"A.J., I want you to wait in the car."

"I'm not some civilian. I'm coming!"

Cal faced her, grabbing her at the shoulders. "You're right; you're not a civilian. You're smart, so tell me, how much training have you had taking down a hostile building?"

She shook her head; she knew he was right. An ass, but right. She walked to the driver's side and got in, checking to confirm the keys were in the ignition. A.J. adjusted the rearview mirror to be able to view the men and the building. She heard the distinctive chirp of her sat phone. *Shit!* It *would* have to be on the floorboard on the passenger side. She'd leaned over the console, stretching and fumbling to get a grip on the phone when she heard a *ping*. Pieces of glass bounced off the dash, falling around her. *What the hell?*

She sat up and instantly saw a spider web of broken glass in the windshield around a hole her fist would pass through. One look in the rearview mirror revealed a small hole about the size of a fucking bullet in the back glass. Then she heard gunfire, lots of it. Had she not bent to reach for the sat phone, the round would have transited her head on the way through the car. No time to see how the gunfight behind her was proceeding. She started the car. Straight ahead, in the wall of the rusted galvanized shop, was an open garage door. As she floored the car, still lying across the console, a second bullet shattered the rearview mirror.

The Toyota skidded through the opening, knocking the side mirror off as it passed through the opening. The interior of the building was unlit; her eyes hadn't adjusted, so she slammed on the brakes and shut down the Toyota. Turning on the headlights, she exited the car. She ran back to the door and peered around the corner. Two CIA guys were pumping rounds into the second floor windows; maybe her would-be assassin was up there. Meanwhile, Cal's men had just kicked in the door and thrown a flash-band grenade inside. She realized then that Cal had been right. Taking down a building was a carefully choreographed dance, each man having a job and all depending on each other for their lives. Dammit, Cal was 100 percent right. She would have been a liability, but here she was, already in the shop. She turned around, scoping out what the car headlights revealed.

A mere five meters in front of the Toyota sat a blue Air Force Jeep, probably the one Roberto had used to deliver the package. Also probably stolen. For some reason, her instincts told her to drop, to crawl. She crawled to the Toyota, opened the passenger door, and retrieved her Beretta. The message light on the phone was blinking. It would freakin' wait. She eased away from the car, working toward the wall. The bare concrete was nasty; hell, the whole building was nasty. It reeked of rat shit, urine, and…perfume. Isobel's perfume.

As A.J.'s eyes adjusted, she continued to ease into the dark space. Her senses were conflicted. Her ears strained to hear any sound, any nuance in the warehouse, all the while hearing gunfire outside. She sensed a presence in the building, but what specifically told her that escaped her. The metal building emitted pops and creaks from the heat.

There! Dead ahead she saw a chair. It looked just like the one in the Polaroid. Duct tape was still attached to the arms, and there was a roll of tape on the floor by the chair, as well as barbed wire. A.J. crawled to the chair. The wire… that was what had bothered her about the photograph. She picked it up and felt several of the barbs. They were dull, filed.

A.J. had grown up on a farm; she had repaired barbed wire fencing with the farm manager and her dad too. Even with gloves, just looking at barbed wire had always resulted in blood, somewhere. Therein was the problem. Isobel's nude body had been wrapped with barbed wire, and there hadn't been a drop of blood, not even a red mark or a scratch. The whole kidnapping had to be a hoax. Isobel was the bait, and A.J. had taken it.

"Welcome, Señorita DeJesus."

Anna whipped around, 9 mm in hand. Carlos stood twenty meters away, Isobel in front of him. Carlos's left arm was around her neck, his right hand holding a pistol to Isobel's head. Isobel was butt naked, her arms behind her.

"I told you to come alone, *puta*."

"You told me Roberto would be alone, Carlos. You gave me your word. So, I'm here, you're here. Why don't you let Isobel go? You have no further use for her."

"You would shoot me where I stand, Anna. Since you've chosen to bring your friends, I need Isobel for my escape, my insurance, no?"

"Carlos, I can offer you insurance. Let her go, we can make a deal."

"That would be most unfortunate for your friend, Anna. She would die."

"Carlos, put your gun down and let Isobel go. You can both live." A.J. had noted the shooting had stopped. She thought Cal would be hunting her; they could already be in the warehouse. The car headlights would make it nearly impossible for Carlos to see behind A.J. She had the upper hand. She could still wind up dead, but by God she had the upper hand.

"Anna, I beg you," Isobel pleaded. "Put your gun down so Carlos can escape. I promise you he won't hesitate to kill me."

A.J. mentally ignored her. She may have been a friend, but now she was an intelligence leak, a traitor, and totally irrelevant. "Carlos, you're under arrest. The only choice you have in this matter is whether you leave this building alive or dead."

"You want me to kill Isobel then?"

"All that will do is insure that you die. The choice is yours, asshole." A.J.'s mind whirled with all the possibilities, moves and countermoves all spinning through her head. She had to end it. She had hoped Carlos would get mad enough to take his weapon away from Isobel's head. There was no reason for Isobel to die if it could be avoided, but Carlos hadn't taken the bait. A.J made her decision.

She allowed the Beretta to drop slightly, as though she intended to drop it. She saw what she was looking for, an almost imperceptible relaxation in Carlos's trigger finger. Even his arm and neck muscles seemed to loosen ever so slightly. A.J. made her move.

She brought the Beretta to bear and fired. Her aiming point was just below the collarbone, Isobel's collarbone.

Isobel looked at A.J. in shock as her knees collapsed. Carlos looked shocked as well because the nine-millimeter round had transited Isobel's body and penetrated Carlos's sternum and his heart. He fell backward to the floor; his pistol fell from his hand. Isobel collapsed in a heap face down on the floor. As A.J. had suspected, Isobel's hands weren't bound. It had been a fake, all of it.

A.J. crossed the distance between them quickly and kicked Carlos's pistol away from him. He looked up at her, and their eyes met, just as his eyes went void of life.

"Fuck, Anna! You fucking shot me. You could've killed me!"

A.J. turned to Isobel. "You're right, I could've." She wheeled, hearing a noise behind her. It was Cal and another contract operator. "Cal, have you got a zip tie?"

"Yeah, what's up?

"Zip her hands. She's the leak and a traitor. Can someone call a medic?" She turned back to Isobel as Cal zipped her hands in front of her. "Why, Isobel? You betrayed us all, Tom, me, all of us. You helped lure me here. Did you think Carlos just wanted to talk?"

Isobel sobbed. "I know. It was the money, it was always the money. At first it was Roberto. He paid me ten grand a month to feed him anything I heard Tom say. After you got here and pissed Carlos off, he was offering a million dollars. A million! I was supposed to kill you the other day. I couldn't do it. Then he offered me a hundred grand just to help lure you here. I'm so sorry, Anna."

"Can you handle her, Cal? I can't deal with even looking at her. How did we come out? Your leg is bleeding."

"We'll handle her. And it went okay. We had two minor injuries, and the bad guys have two dead and two in custody, not counting these two."

"When did you guys come in?"

"Just before you shot. We had your back, but there wasn't really anything we could have done any differently."

She nodded, turned, and walked back to the car to retrieve her sat phone. The display showed that T.D. had called. He answered almost instantly. "Hey, T.D."

"Hey, sis. It's Isobel. When we ran her through the computers, they lit up like a Christmas tree. Her voice is tied to Roberto, going back for months."

A.J. saw no reason to burst his bubble. "Okay. That's what I thought, but I had to know. Thanks, brother. By the way, I'm taking your advice; I'm tired. I'm out of here."

"Good! I've gotta go, you okay?"

"Yeah, I'll be fine. Out."

Chapter 29

Howard AFB

Balboa, Panama

"So, where are you headed?" Tom asked.

He and A.J. were standing in front of an Air Force transport plane. A.J. sported an entirely new outfit—jeans, boots, shirt, and sports jacket. A shoulder holster helped hide the nine-mm Beretta; a DEA badge was clipped to her belt. It was the first time since she had gone to work for Tom she had worn her "real" uniform.

She smiled. "Sorry, that's classified."

"Touché, okay, take your vacation. You've earned it. Here, the guys and I wanted to give you something, a bonus so to speak." He handed her a fat envelope.

A.J. looked inside; it was stuffed with Benjamin's.

"Tom, I can't take this."

"A.J., like I said, you've earned it. Contractually, if you bothered to read it, you were entitled to one all-expense paid vacation per year. Besides, all this week, you were supposed to be on medical leave. By the way, I understand your reasons, but I'm hurt you called for Cal and the others and left me out of the loop."

"I know, I didn't want to do it, but I was afraid Isobel had gone rogue, and I knew the two of you had a relationship. You would feel torn, and shit, I could've been wrong."

"But you weren't. It was a huge error in judgment on my part. How did you know."

"I wasn't positive for a long time. She seemed to be the only person that could have known what we all found had leaked. I didn't want to believe it. Since the two of you were, well, close, I figure you would refuse to believe me. When T.D. told me her voice was definitely tied to Carlos by phone calls I had my proof. By then, I'd already shot her and Carlos."

"You could've made a huge mistake. You could've killed her. It all could've been a huge mistake."

"People make mistakes, Tom. I know I have. Don't let it get to you. Shit happens."

Tom sighed. "It's time for you to board. This plane runs to Laughlin Air Force Base in Texas every few days. Thought you'd like not having to go through customs. Can I carry your bag for you?"

"Nah, boss, I've got it." She tried to hand the envelope back to Tom.

"Look, it's yours either way. Take it, or I deposit it in your offshore account. You saved a lot of lives, you helped snatch some big cash and drugs, and you put down a rabid dog. You earned it." He tried to hug her but was greeted by a stiffened torso on A.J.'s part. "I…I'm sorry…"

"Tom. It's not you; it's me. I'm sorry, you did nothing wrong." She extended her hand. He shook it firmly. She picked up her bag and turned to go and then felt a firm swat to her ass. “That’s better.” She laughed. She walked up the steps and let an airman escort her to a seat. She looked out the window and waved at Tom. He returned the wave, turned, and walked away.

Twelve hours and two Delta flights later, A.J. shut down her rental car and got out. She left the keys in the car but did grab her briefcase; it had several guns in it. She thought the car would be safe; after all, she was in what she considered to be a pretty damned secure area.

She ran through a chilly rain up to a well-camouflaged steel door painted to look like an old wood door and knocked. She had a key somewhere, but right now, she wasn’t sure where it was.

The door opened. An attractive woman in a sweatshirt and jeans stood on the threshold.

“Hi, Mom, I’m home.”

“Oh my God, Alexandra! I had no idea! Don’t stand out there. Come in and let me give you a hug!” Samantha grabbed A.J. and forcibly dragged her into the foyer. “Let me look at you. My God, A.J., you’re a grown woman.” Sam opened A.J.’s jacket. “You’re a freakin’ cop. Gun, badge, the whole nine yards. Please let’s go to the kitchen. I’ve got spaghetti on the stove. Your dad will be home any time. Why didn’t you call to tell us you were coming?”

“Mom, it’s been, well, exciting. I’ve been doing some very classified work.”

“In Colombia, right? That was the last Thomas Hendrix told us.”

“Well, I *was* in Colombia. That’s where I got shot, and then I was in Panama…”

“Shot? Mary Mother of Jesus; A.J., you were shot? Holy shit!”

“Mother, it hit me in the vest, not a drop of blood. It just kicked me like a pissed-off mule, but enough of that. I know this’ll be a shock, but wanna know what I’d really like?”

“Anything, dear, it’s yours.”

“I’d really like a hug, and a drink. In that order.”

Sam had a smile on her face as she hunted a bottle of Crown and two glasses. Steve walked in halfway through the second glass for A.J. He whistled his way in the front door asking, “Sam, whose rental car is out…” when he was assaulted by a young woman wearing a gun. The next fifteen minutes were spent with A.J. sharing what she felt comfortable telling her parents about what had gone on throughout the year since her last trip home.

“A.J., excuse me just a moment. If you don’t mind, I’d like to call some people. We need to have a party. I need to get T.D. over here.”

“Uh, Dad, don’t think that’s gonna happen. He’s out of town. Way, way out of town.”

Steve laughed. “Okay, I guess I should have seen it coming.”

“What’s that, hubby of mine?”

“The day when everything our little children did was classified!” The room filled with laughter. Steve headed for his office to get on the phone.

Dinner was a happy occasion, preceded by a heartfelt prayer by Samantha. After dinner, they moved to the sitting room, and being the provocateur she was, Samantha began.

“So, how about you tell your father about getting shot.”

“Mom…”

“Shot?”

Sam was enjoying this; she loved controversy.

"Okay, I guess. So, I was twenty feet up in this tree with a highly modified M-16 with a sight and suppressor. My assignment was to prevent vehicles from leaving a specific site—"

Her dad interrupted. "Where were you?"

A.J. smiled. "I'm sorry, I can't tell you that. Anyway, there was a pickup with a Russian light machine gun mounted in the back. I saw that gun as a serious threat, so I stopped it by taking out the driver first, then I—"

"Do you mean you killed someone?" Samantha asked.

"Yeah, Mom, and he wasn't the first, and just so you know, I think the Zippo actually did help."

Steve jumped in now. "Zippo?"

"Just continue," Sam said, doing her best to redirect the conversation.

"Yeah, so anyway, by the time I got the truck stopped, the machine gun operator had spotted me. I could see his eyes when I pulled the trigger. Unfortunately, he got a burst of 7.62 off at me. I took one square in the chest."

"What? A 7.62? I'm glad I'm wrong, but a vest won't stop a 7.62 square on. You should be dead. Sorry, Sam." Steve's wife was staring at him with a look of horror on her face. "Well, it's true."

"Yeah, you're right, Dad, but the people I work for buy the good stuff. The vest had one of those heavy ceramic plates in it. Still kicked my ass though. My chest still looks like I was in a car wreck."

Sam had caught what the reporter side of her thought sounded like a line of questioning. "You said the people you work for, but you work for the DEA, don't you?"

“Mom, Dad, here’s the deal. I can tell you a little about what I’ve been up to, but where and, most especially, who my actual employers are? That’s totally off limits.”

Her dad nodded. “I understand, so how long can you stay?”

“A week. Maybe two. I had to get away for a while.”

Steve nodded, he was obviously thinking of several things at once. “Well, there will certainly be a picnic here tomorrow, right, dear?”

Sam agreed totally. “We’ll take care of everything. You look tired dear; I’ll go make up your bed. Okay?”

A.J. nodded; she was tired. Actually, she was exhausted. She and Steve went to the rental car and gathered the rest of her gear and headed upstairs. Sam was gone, grabbing bedding. Her dad placed the duffel bag on the floor, and A.J. dropped her briefcase on the bed.

“Here, Dad, I wanted to show you something.” She opened the lizard-skinned case, set the paperwork aside, and opened the false bottom. “It’s kinda like your Halliburton case, Dad.”

Steve whistled and picked up the Beretta. He returned it and carefully pulled the .22 with the suppressor out. “This one tells me you do some very close work.” He returned it to the case. “So, my daughter is a full-fledged assassin, am I correct?”

“’Fraid so, Dad.”

He nodded. “Well, your mom was right; it terrifies me. It’s not a long-term career. You do realize that, right?”

A.J. nodded. “I can see that.”

Ten minutes later, she was in her bed. She fell asleep almost instantly.

The next morning they were enjoying breakfast when the phone rang. Samantha answered it. “Hello? T.D.! How are you, son? That's great. Guess who's sitting at the kitchen table right now. How did you know? I've been hearing that expression a lot lately. Where are you? Classified, huh? Okay, been hearing that a lot too. Sure, I'll get her. Your brother wants to talk to you, A.J."

"Hey, T.D., how in the hell did you know where I was? I didn't tell a soul."

"I'm NSA, remember, sis?"

"Right. So what's up? When are you going to be able to leave? Think Kevin will let you go?"

"Soon, a couple of days I think. We're still wrapping up the intel from your last op. That's why I'm calling. I've got some bad news. Can you talk?

A.J. looked at her parents at the table. "Give me a minute. Can I take this call in your office?"

"Sure, honey, go pick up in there, and I'll hang up."

A few moments later, A.J. picked up the phone at her dad's desk. She listened for the click of her dad hanging up the kitchen phone and proceeded. "So what's the bad news, brother?"

"It's Carlos, he's not dead. The guy you offed in the warehouse was a double. His prints don't match, and there were definite signs of some excellent plastic surgery."

"Shit! I thought it was over. Guess not. How's Isobel?"

"She'll recover. Tom hasn't decided what to do with her yet, but she's going to jail somewhere. Tom said to tell you she wanted you to know she's sorry, that it wasn't personal."

"It never is. I guess this is one of those times when my inability to become attached to people comes in handy."

"Guess so, sis. Anyway I'll call back if I learn more. Enjoy your vacation. Sorry if I ruined it, but I thought you needed to know."

"It's okay. Take care of yourself and tell all the guys thanks for everything." A.J. walked back to the kitchen.

"What's wrong, dear?" her dad asked. "You look disappointed."

A.J. simply looked at her parents. No appropriate words came to her.

"Classified, dear?" Sam asked.

A.J. nodded, sat down at the table, and resumed breakfast.

The picnic went well. Linda, Hendrix, and Chrissy and her husband showed. Frank, the farm manager, and his wife and grandkids made it too. They all sat around the pool and enjoyed burgers and the normal picnic side dishes. Hendrix entertained with his side of how A.J.'s Article 32 hearing had gone, leaving out the parts involving potential national security issues.

The next week flew by. Sam and Steve totally abandoned their jobs to spend time with their daughter. On Sunday, the three loaded up in Samantha's 5 series BMW and drove to the little Catholic Church in Fredericksburg. A.J. found some appropriate clothing in her closet. She sat between her parents thinking that Sam, maybe Steve too, would have had a minor stroke had they known there was a nine mm Beretta in her purse. A.J. had become so used to carrying a weapon anywhere she went she hadn't even thought about it until she moved her purse to the floor between the pews.

She swam, they fished in the creek, and her parents ran with her. Sam had looked horrified the first time she saw the mixture of purple and greenish bruises still on A.J.'s chest. Her dad had actually grinned and told Sam the bruise was both a badge of courage and a reminder not to get in the way of a bullet again. A.J. could see the look of pride in Steve's face.

A.J. enjoyed the time. At the same time, she gradually realized as her mind decompressed that, as pleasant as the time was, the farm was no longer her home. She had moved on, in many ways. She was getting antsy.

Wednesday morning, she was sitting at the kitchen table as Sam spoke to Chrissy on the phone when Mr. Frank walked in the back door.

"I picked up the mail, Miss Samantha," he announced, depositing the stack on the table in front of Sam. "How are you this morning, Alexandra?" Frank loved to tease A.J. with that. For some reason, she allowed him to get away with it.

Sam nodded and smiled at Frank as she continued with Chrissy. She flipped through the mail, completed her call, and stopped on one letter. "Who the hell is Anna DeJesus?"

"That's mine, Mom," A.J. replied as she grabbed the letter and Sam's letter opener. The outside of the envelope was handwritten, had no return address, and had Colombian stamps all over it. Inside was a single sheet of paper, also handwritten in Spanish.

Puta – This isn't over. Carlos

A wadded piece of paper bounced off the wall.

The End

Please take this opportunity to read a "sneak peek" of the beginning of the next book in the Deadlier Than the Male series. The Queen of Spades

Fredericksburg Virginia

"Why are you packing?" Samantha stood in her daughter's bedroom watching A.J. stuff clothing into a duffel bag. "Does this have something to do with that letter?"

"Yes, Mom, it has *everything* to do with the letter. Without going into details, there's a very bad man in Colombia my employers and I have serious issues with. In all honesty, I thought I had killed him just before I left to come here. I didn't tell a soul where I was headed, not even T.D. Well, the asshole has found me, God help me if I know how. I've got to go, immediately."

"Are you afraid he'll come after you here? In the States?"

"Partly, but honestly what I'm concerned about is you and Dad. My being here has placed you in danger, and I couldn't live with myself if that animal did anything to you two."

"Your father and I are not helpless. We have resources."

"Mother, you have no idea what this piece of shit is capable of."

"And you, Alexandra, have forgotten what your parents are capable of. Please humor me. Give me fifteen minutes. If I can't convince you to stay and feel the three of us are safe, I'll help you pack. Deal?"

A.J. looked at her mother and saw a look of determination and strength in Samantha's eyes. She admired her mom, tough as nails when required, but so capable of the love A.J. wished she could duplicate. Right now, she was looking at a determined woman who was not going to take no for an answer.

"Okay, Mom, I don't see you changing my mind, but it's your dime. Convince me."

"Follow me, young lady." Sam spun on her heel and headed down the stairs. She stopped in the kitchen. Samantha grasped the cabinet on the wall and slid it to the side. A.J. knew the contents of the room behind the cabinet; the home's original owner had installed a surveillance system that monitored the entire farm property—TV cameras, microphones, a remotely operated gate—and it was actually a very sophisticated system for a "private" property. The room's existence was no surprise to A.J., but she was greeted when the door opened by a twenty-something-year-old man. It was the farm manager's son, Jacob. He was "manning the board" so to speak, monitoring all the equipment and cameras.

"Hey, Miss Alexandra, how ya doin'?"

"Fine, Jacob, what are you doing here?" A.J. asked. She knew Jacob; he'd been a second brother to her growing up.

"I'm guarding the Moring property, ma'am. Twelve on, twelve off; Dad's got the board when Mom or I don't."

Samantha waved at Jacob and grabbed A.J.'s arm. "Come on, dear, you haven't seen shit yet." She took off out the door, headed for the barn. "Been in the barn since you've been back, daughter?"

"No, why do I suspect there's going to be another surprise, Mother?"

"It's the way we Moring women are, dear. You know that!" Sam slid the heavy door open. "Hey, guys. Everybody good today?"

A.J.'s jaw dropped. In the barn were six guys, and everyone looked like an ex-Marine or Army vet. They were all crew cut and looked like men no one in their right mind would deliberately piss off. There were cots, groceries, and guns. Lots of guns.

A huge black man walked up to Sam. "We're good, Miss Samantha. Gonna introduce us?"

Sam shook his hand. "Yeah, Dewayne, this is A.J. She thinks she's a badass. You two need to compare war stories some time."

Dewayne walked up to A.J. and shook her hand. "A.J., glad to meet you. We've seen you of course. Whenever you've left the house, you've had a tail. There's eighteen of us here, every single one with combat experience and every one of us owes your dad a favor. He called the day you arrived. Took a few days for all of us to get here, but trust me, young lady, ain't no man or men gettin' in here. I can't hardly see how you didn't make us."

"You're right. I'm disappointed in myself, but thank you, all of you. Mom's trying convince me not to leave. I was worried about her and Dad, but I feel a lot better. Can I come back later and visit?"

The entire group nodded and shouted a group, "Hell yeah!"

"Let's go back to the house. There's more I need to tell you about." Samantha dragged A.J. by the arm, and the two headed back toward the house. “You know, we’ve been residents of Fredericksburg for over twenty years now, dear. As of right now, the entire town is on high alert for anyone that even smells different, out of the ordinary. The police, sheriff’s department, private citizens, all of them have our backs. We couldn’t be much safer if we were in the middle of Quantico.”

The two walked into the kitchen. “Sit,” Sam directed, motioning A.J. to the table. “Okay, dear, I think I’ve shown you your father and I are safe. So, what’s next?”

A.J. regrouped. What had been of supreme importance to her ten minutes earlier was now secondary. “Well, first, how did the ass find out where I am? Second, I need to find him and kill him, again.”

Sam nodded. “Let’s get going on the first one. Do we call Linda and our FBI friends?”

“It couldn’t hurt, Mom, but actually T.D. is the key. He found me unless he just played a hunch. Somehow, he told somebody. I’m going to call T.D. and Tom. That’s where I’m starting.”

“Okay, dear. Your dad’s at Quantico today anyway. I’m calling him while you make your calls.

A.J. went upstairs and got out the sat phone. “Hey, Tom, it’s A.J.”

“A.J., how are you?”

“I’m good. Well, I promised I’d check in once I got where I was going. How’s things on your end?”

“Fine, fine. Where are you? Somewhere by a pool sipping a piña colada I hope.”

“Actually I’m on a farm outside D.C., and I need your help.”

“Sure, what can I do?”

"T.D. called me here within twenty-four hours of my arrival. I was a little surprised he found me, but not upset. What upset me was the love note I got from Carlos this morning in the mail."

"Holy crap! That's bad, girl, very bad. You leaving?"

"No, long story, but let's say my Mom and Dad are not without friends and resources. What I need though is for you and T.D. to put your heads together. Somehow Carlos found me through him. It makes no sense to me, but unless Carlos has some direct line to Jesus, I should have been a ghost. I paid cash for my plane tickets; I used throwaway ID's all that shit. So, please, get with T.D. and have him call me."

"Got it. I'll get started right away."

"One more thing Tom. Find the bastard. When you do, I'm coming back. I've never had to kill someone twice, but it couldn't happen to a nicer guy. If you miss me, find him. I can be there in twenty-four hours."

"Got it. We'll get him. We all will. See you soon, and be careful."

"You too. Out." She tossed the sat phone on the bed. *You're staying dead this time, Carlos.*

ABOUT THE AUTHOR

Donald lives a quiet life in North Florida with his wife. They both have "real" jobs, a grown daughter, and grandchildren. As a mystery writer, he feels some mystery about the author is a good thing; besides, your concept of what he's like could be a lot more exciting than the reality.

If you feel you simply must know more about the author, please visit Donald Churchwell Books on facebook. Roam around, "Like" the page. You will get updates on works in progress, and you'll be the first to know when something new is coming out.

One more thing. Donald wanted to share what he *isn't.* He's not an ex Seal, Ranger, Marine Recon, or any of that really cool stuff. Nor did he ever work for one of those alphabet agencies. So anything you read as he weaves his fictional characters through history is just the product of a twisted mind, and could never have *really* happened. Honest.

Made in the USA
Middletown, DE
01 December 2021

53964065R00146